Leadership According To the Apostle John

Leadership Legacy and Guiding Principles for Today

Giulio Veglio

Dedication

I would like to begin this dedication by expressing my heartfelt gratitude to all those who have supported and guided me throughout my life. Your presence and influence have been invaluable, and I am truly grateful for your contributions.

However, as I reflect upon the journey that has led me to this moment, I am compelled to dedicate this book to a higher power. This dedication belongs to God, who has been my constant protector and watchful presence every single day. In times of need, His guidance and unwavering love have sustained me.

I also dedicate this book to Jesus, God's only begotten son, who was sent to us to teach, save, and ultimately sacrifice Himself on the cross. His blood was shed for the forgiveness of our sins, and on the third day, He triumphantly rose again, now seated at the right hand of His Father. Jesus, thank you for the inspiration and wisdom you have bestowed upon me, enabling me to serve others and fulfill your will.

May this book serve as a testament to the grace and mercy of God, and may it inspire others to seek His guidance and embrace His love. To God and Jesus, I offer my deepest gratitude and devotion.

Acknowledgment

First and foremost, I extend my deepest appreciation to the Apostle John for his timeless wisdom and insights, which serve as the foundation of this work.

I am indebted to my mentors and advisors whose guidance and encouragement have been invaluable throughout this journey.

I am also grateful to my family and friends for their patience, understanding, and belief in me.

Lastly, I acknowledge the readers whose interest and engagement inspire me to continue exploring and sharing these transformative principles.

Thank you all for being a part of this endeavor.

Giulio Veglio

CONTENTS

About the Author

Giulio Veglio stands as a testament to the transformative power of leadership and service. Beginning his illustrious career with John Paul Mitchell Systems in 1984, he swiftly advanced from an enterprising salon owner to an internationally recognized educator and master stylist. His innovative approaches to customer service have propelled multiple salons and educational institutions to the forefront of the industry.

As a Harvard Business School Executive MBA graduate and a certified Maxwell Leadership Executive, Trainer, Speaker, and Coach, Veglio embodies a lifetime commitment to personal development and empowerment. His accolades, including the 2023 Outstanding Leadership Award and the 2024 Visionary Award, underscore his significant impact on global education and business.

Veglio's influence extends beyond the boardroom into the heart of communities through his philanthropic efforts, raising over $25M annually for varied causes. His bilingual fluency and rich cultural experiences, spanning from Italy to the US, have enriched his engagements with diverse audiences around the world.

An ordained minister and a staunch advocate against human trafficking, Veglio's life work resonates with profound empathy and a relentless drive for societal betterment. His literary contributions further this legacy and Award winning books, with titles such as "A Slap on the Back of the Head" and Unwrapping Your Gifts. reflecting his passion for guiding others to uncover their potential.

As an Italian immigrant who embraced US citizenship with pride, Giulio Veglio continues to illuminate paths for others, whether through his stirring oration or through the written word, leaving indelible marks of inspiration across continents.

Introduction:

The Leadership Legacy of John: Guiding Principles for Today

In the realm of leadership, few figures in history possess the profound influence and timeless wisdom of John. His life and teachings, chronicled in the biblical book bearing his name, continue to resonate with people across generations and cultures. From his unwavering commitment to truth and compassion to his remarkable ability to inspire and guide others, John's leadership legacy serves as a guiding light, illuminating the path for leaders in the present day.

The Book of John opens a window into the life of this extraordinary individual, revealing the core principles that shaped both his character and his approach to leadership. Through his intimate connection with Jesus Christ, John learned pivotal lessons about humility, courage, and sacrificial love—the cornerstones of authentic leadership. Although his experiences were rooted in a distant era, the profound wisdom found in his words transcends time, offering invaluable insights for leaders navigating the complexities of the modern world.

John's teachings serve as an invitation to explore the depths of our own leadership potential. As we delve into the pages of his book, we encounter profound truths that challenge us to examine our motives, refine our character, and cultivate the virtues necessary for effective leadership. His words resound with clarity and conviction, piercing through the noise of the contemporary world, and reminding us of the eternal truths that underpin meaningful leadership.

Throughout this journey, we will uncover the profound impact of John's leadership principles on our personal and professional lives. We will explore his unwavering commitment to truth, his relentless pursuit of justice, and his unwavering faith in the transformative power of love. Drawing from his words, we will discover practical strategies to foster trust, inspire vision, and create an environment conducive to growth and flourishing.

As we delve into the life and teachings of John, we will also encounter his remarkable capacity for empathy and compassion. In a world often characterized by division and discord, John's example calls us to embrace our shared humanity and extend grace to those around us. His words remind us that leadership is not a mere exercise of authority but a sacred responsibility to serve and uplift others.

In the following chapters, we will delve into the timeless wisdom of John, exploring how his teachings can be applied to the challenges and opportunities faced by leaders in the 21st century. We will examine his profoundinsight into the nature of leadership, drawing from both his biblical quotes and the broader context of his life and

Chapter 1
Becoming the Light

My story of how I related to becoming the light:

Once upon a time, in the early years of my life, I was the radiant beacon of joy and happiness in my family. As a child, my heart radiated with boundless light that touched the hearts of those around me. However, this brilliance was soon to face a formidable challenge as I ventured into the world of elementary school.

Being an Italian immigrant with no knowledge of the English language, I was plunged into a world of incomprehension. The words spoken around me were gibberish, and the lessons in the classroom seemed like an enigma. First grade brought with it not only a new grade but also the harsh reality of being held back, unable to read, write, or truly understand.

As I grappled with my struggles, a more sinister force began to emerge in my life: bullying. It wasn't just my fellow students who tormented me but some teachers as well. They pulled my hair, slapped me, and subjected me to a barrage of hurtful words, branding me as "stupid," "dumb," and "useless." It was at this juncture that my inner light began to flicker and fade.

It was only after high school, despite still grappling with illiteracy, that I stumbled upon the guiding lights of my life – mentors who recognized my hidden talents. These mentors, with their wisdom and knowledge, began to nurture the faintest spark within me.

With their guidance, I embarked on a journey of self-discovery and skill mastery, eventually finding my calling in hair styling. As my mentors continued to shower me with their support and knowledge, my inner light began to shine brighter with each passing day.

In my early twenties, as I honed my craft, I felt a burning desire to help others like me. I wanted to use my newfound brilliance to lead others out of the darkness I had once known so intimately. The more I learned and shared with others, the brighter my own light became.

As I evolved into an educator, I found myself traveling the world, illuminating the lives of countless individuals. My light no longer served my ego but was drawn from the depths of my heart. I realized that my influence could transform lives not only in my craft but also in business and, most importantly, in faith.

Today, I pray fervently that God continues to bless me with the gift to help others find their own inner light and kindle their flames. My hope is that they, too, will pass the torch, sharing their light to guide others out of darkness.

The story of my journey from a dimly lit existence to becoming a guiding light for others underscores a profound truth: No matter how dark life may become, our inner light can always be rekindled with great faith and the guidance of compassionate leaders.

In illuminating the lives of others, we not only find our purpose but also create a ripple effect that helps countless souls find their own path to enlightenment. Leadership is not about ego or power but about using our light to lead others towards their own brilliance, creating a world where the darkness can never truly extinguish the flame of hope and inspiration.

"In the depths of darkness, even the faintest spark can become a blazing beacon. With faith and the guidance of compassionate leaders, we have the power to rekindle our own light and, in doing so, ignite the flames of hope in others." Quote Giulio Veglio

****

In a world often consumed by darkness, confusion, and uncertainty, the idea of being a light may seem like an elusive and distant concept. Yet, within the pages of the book of John, we find a profound invitation to become the light that illuminates the path for others.

In this chapter, we will explore the significance of being the light according to the book of John and how it applies to us personally and as leaders who influence others professionally in today's world. We will draw inspiration from the timeless wisdom of John's Gospel, delving into his words and discovering the transformative power they hold.

The Call to Shine:

John 8:12: "Again, Jesus spoke to them, saying,

"I am the light of the world. Whoever follows me will not walk in darkness but will have the light of life."

From the very beginning, John establishes Jesus as the ultimate source of light, the beacon that guides us through the darkness of our lives. Jesus invites us to follow Him, embrace His teachings, and immerse ourselves in the radiance of His love.

Through this divine connection, we are transformed into vessels of light capable of illuminating the lives of others. In a world yearning for hope, compassion, and understanding, we are called to be the reflection of Christ's light.

Embracing our identity:

John 1:4-5: "In him was life, and the life was the light of men. The light shines in the darkness, and the darkness has not overcome it."

As we delve deeper into John's Gospel, we encounter the profound truth that life itself is intertwined with light. We are not mere bystanders in this cosmic dance of illumination.

Instead, we are intricately connected to the light, and it is our duty to let it shine through us. By acknowledging our identity as carriers of the divine light, we relinquish the shackles of self-doubt and embrace our purpose as beacons of hope, love, and truth.

Personal Transformation:

John 3:19-20: "And this is the judgment: the light has come into the world, and people loved the darkness rather than the light because their works were evil. For everyone who does wicked things hates the light and does not come to the light, lest his works should be exposed."

John's words remind us that our journey toward becoming the light requires personal transformation. It necessitates a sincere examination of our own hearts, a willingness to confront our own darkness, and a commitment to align our actions with the principles of righteousness. By allowing the light of Christ to penetrate the depths of our being, we embark on a transformative journey that not only brings personal fulfillment but also radiates outward, touching the lives of those around us.

Leadership and Influence:

John 13:15: "For I have given you an example, that you also should do just as I have done to you."

As leaders in today's world, our capacity to be the light expands beyond our personal lives. Our influence extends to those we lead, to the teams, organizations, and communities we serve. John's Gospel challenges us to lead by example and to embody the qualities of compassion, humility, and servant leadership that Jesus exemplified. By embracing our role as leaders who illuminate the way for others, we inspire and empower those around us to discover their own light and potential.

Your true calling is "To Be the light."

Exercise 1

How will you start Embracing your own Light Within?

Call to Action:

Recognize the divine spark within yourself and commit to nurturing it for personal and professional growth.

If you wish to Read and meditate on John 1:4-5, reflect on the following questions:

1. How does John describe Jesus as the "light of all mankind"?

2. In what ways can you tap into the light within yourself, which is a reflection of Christ's presence?

3. How can you cultivate personal growth and transformation by allowing Christ's light to shine through your thoughts, attitudes, and actions?

Call to Action

Take time each day for self-reflection and introspection. Identify areas where you can let your light shine brighter and commit to personal growth and transformation.

Exercise 2

How can you Radiate the Light that shines within you to Others?

Call to Action:

Extend the light of Christ to others by embodying His teachings and serving as an example of love and compassion.

If you wish, Read and reflect on John 13:34-35.

Consider the following questions:

1. How does Jesus command His followers to love one another?

2. In what ways can you demonstrate love and compassion to your team members and colleagues?

3. How can you create a positive and uplifting environment that reflects the light of Christ within your professional sphere?

Call to Action

Purposefully seek opportunities to extend love, kindness, and support to others in your personal and professional circles.

Aim to create an atmosphere where others can experience the transformative power of Christ's love.

Chapter 2

The Wisdom of John and Its Application in Today's World

In the book of John, we find profound words of wisdom that remind us of the eternal truth that there is always someone wiser and smarter to come. John's teachings not only hold spiritual significance but also offer valuable insights for our personal growth and professional leadership in the modern world. Let us explore how these teachings apply to us individually and as leaders who influence others.

John 3:30 states,

"He must increase, but I must decrease."

These words encapsulate the essence of humility and the recognition that our knowledge and abilities are limited. As individuals, we often strive for personal growth and success. However, John reminds us that true wisdom lies in acknowledging our limitations and embracing the wisdom and guidance of others. By humbling ourselves, we create space for new knowledge and perspectives to enrich our lives.

As leaders, the application of John's teachings becomes even more critical. In today's fast-paced and ever-changing world, effective leadership demands a willingness to learn and adapt.

John 13:15 advises,

"For I have given you an example, that you also should do just as I have done to you."

A leader who seeks to influence others professionally must display the humility to learn from those around them, including their subordinates. By doing so, they create an environment that encourages growth and collaboration, ultimately leading to the success of the entire team.

Furthermore, John 14:26 reminds us of the Holy Spirit, described as the Helper, who will teach and guide us. Applying this to our professional lives, we can foster a culture of continuous learning and mentorship. As leaders, we can guide and inspire others to seek knowledge and wisdom beyond our own.

By encouraging our team members to learn from diverse sources, we help them develop their own unique perspectives and skills. In doing so, we create a legacy that surpasses our individual contributions.

In conclusion, the teachings of John offer timeless wisdom applicable to both our personal lives and professional roles as leaders. By embracing humility and recognizing that there is always someone wiser and smarter to come, we open ourselves to growth and progress.

As leaders, we must foster a culture of learning and mentorship, guiding others to surpass us in knowledge and skills.

To put these teachings into action, I encourage you to reflect on your leadership style,

Call to Action

1. **Embrace Humility:** Recognize and acknowledge your limitations. Understand that there is always more to learn and discover.

2. **Seek Mentors:** Surround yourself with individuals who possess wisdom and experience beyond your own. Learn from them and allow their guidance to shape your leadership.

3. **Foster a Learning Culture:** Encourage your team members to pursue continuous learning and personal growth. Provide opportunities for mentorship and create an environment that values diverse perspectives and knowledge.

4. **Empower Others:** Actively support and promote the development of your team members. Encourage them to rise to leadership positions and guide them in their journey towards replacing you.

Remember, true leadership lies not in the desire to hold power but in the ability to inspire and empower others. By embracing the wisdom of John, we can become transformative leaders who leave a lasting impact on those we influence.

Chapter 3
Communication and Listening

My Story

From a young age, I always considered myself a great communicator. I could talk my way out of trouble and passionately share my ideas with anyone who would listen.

However, I couldn't help but wonder why people didn't take me seriously. They would offer advice, but I was often too busy talking or getting distracted. You see, I am an individual with ADD and ADHD, and my enthusiasm sometimes felt boundless, to the point where it may have seemed like I was on overdrive.

One day, I had the opportunity to speak with John Paul DeJoria, the co-owner of John Paul Mitchell Systems and the well-known Patron Tequila brand. He expressed a desire to invest in me by purchasing a building for a school in New York, offering me a 50% ownership stake with no initial financial burden. However, my ADD kicked in, and I started to overtalk and lose focus on what he wanted to do for me.

My excitement got the best of me, and I became distracted by others in the room, even welcoming friends mid-conversation. Regrettably, I didn't notice when he politely walked away. It was a missed opportunity that taught me a valuable lesson I now share with many.

The lesson is this: communication is not just about speaking but also about listening and connecting. That day, I lost more than an opportunity; I missed out on the invaluable knowledge and wisdom he was willing to impart, particularly about the significance of ownership versus leasing. I eventually apologized to him for my rudeness, not because I wanted his investment but because it was the right thing to do.

While we never became real estate partners, our friendship remained strong. When he speaks, I listen and learn, then ask questions. Since that day, my world has become much clearer. I've discovered that through listening, I gain a deeper understanding and can connect more effectively with others.

My leadership has ascended to new heights, and my understanding of God, Jesus, and faith has deepened as I embrace the wisdom of listening, just as God and Jesus have modeled for us.

Profound Main Point

In the art of communication, the greatest lesson I've learned is that it's not about how much we speak but how effectively we listen and connect with others. The ability to truly listen with compassion, love, and empathy can transform our relationships, leadership, and understanding of the world. It is a lesson that mirrors the example set by God and Jesus, who walk among us through the practice of active, attentive listening.

Personal Quote

"Effective communication begins with the art of listening, where understanding takes root, and connections flourish. In the silence of attentive ears, we find the wisdom to speak with purpose, connect with empathy, and lead with heart." - Quote Giulio Veglio

In this chapter, we will explore the profound wisdom found in the book of John regarding effective communication and active listening. We will delve into how these principles apply to us personally and as leaders in today's fast-paced world. By understanding the teachings of John, we can learn how to effectively convey our message and become great listeners, fostering meaningful connections and influencing others professionally.

The Art of Effective Communication

In this chapter, we will explore the profound wisdom found in the book of John regarding effective communication and active listening. We will delve into how these principles apply to us personally and as leaders in today's fast-paced world.

By understanding the teachings of John, we can learn how to effectively convey our message and become great listeners, fostering meaningful connections and influencing others professionally.

In John 1:1, it is stated, "In the beginning was the Word, and the Word was with God, and the Word was God."

This verse reminds us of the power that lies within our words. As leaders, our messages carry weight and impact. It is crucial to choose our words carefully, ensuring they align with our intentions and resonate with our audience. Effective communication involves clarity, authenticity, and empathy.

1. How will you Honor your own voice as well as the Voice of Others?

John 10:27 states,

"My sheep listen to my voice; I know them, and they follow me."

This verse emphasizes the importance of listening in our personal and professional lives. As leaders, we must cultivate the skill of active listening, giving our full attention to others. By honoring their voice, we create an environment of trust and respect, fostering open dialogue and collaboration.

2. How will you overcome Barriers to Communication?

John 8:43 says,

"Why is my language not clear to you? Because you are unable to hear what I say."

This verse highlights the existence of barriers that hinder effective communication. As leaders, we must be aware of these barriers, such as assumptions, biases, and distractions. By actively working to overcome them, we can create a space where our message can be heard and understood by others.

Connecting on a Deeper Level

John 13:34-35 states,

"A new command I give you: Love one another. As I have loved you, so you must love one another. By this, everyone will know that you are my disciples if you love one another."

These verses remind us of the importance of building genuine connections with others. As leaders, we must approach communication and listening with love and compassion. This allows us to connect on a deeper level, fostering trust, loyalty, and respect within our professional relationships.

To be heard by others and become great listeners, we must embrace the teachings of John. By communicating effectively, honoring the voice of others, overcoming communication barriers, and connecting on a deeper level, we can make a profound impact as leaders in today's world. Let us commit to being intentional in our words and actions, fostering an environment where everyone feels valued and heard.

Call to Action

1. **Be Hard by Others:** Strive to be receptive and open-minded when others share their insights, perspectives, and concerns. Value their input and actively seek opportunities to learn from their experiences.

2. **Seek to Understand:** Practice active listening by giving your full attention to others. Seek to understand their viewpoints, emotions, and needs. Empathize with their experiences and validate their feelings.

3. **Connect as a Leader:** Foster a culture of collaboration and connection within your professional sphere. Encourage open dialogue, create safe spaces for honest communication, and prioritize building meaningful relationships with your team members and colleagues.

By embodying the principles of effective communication and active listening, we can become influential leaders who inspire and empower others to reach their full potential.

Chapter 4
See the True Value in Others

My story

In my previous story, I shared the painful experiences of feeling devalued and dismissed by those who failed to recognize my worth. They wrote me off in school, curving my grades and sending me on my way without a second thought. It was as if they couldn't see any value in my existence, and that's precisely why they never took the time to understand my struggles in reading and writing. I excelled in math until the dreaded word problems came along, and then I found myself adrift.

My math teacher in the 10th grade openly humiliated me in front of the entire class, questioning when I had become "stupid" and urging me not to attend his class anymore. Throughout my life, I encountered numerous individuals who devalued and dismissed me, often based solely on appearances or a lack of understanding.

But it was the mentors who saw value in me, who recognized my potential, and who valued my unique strengths that made all the difference. They believed in me when others didn't, and their support became the foundation upon which I built my life. In the example of Jesus and John, we find a profound lesson in seeing the value in every individual, no matter their circumstances.

As leaders, we have a responsibility to see the inherent value in others, to identify their strengths, and to help them cultivate those strengths. God does not make mistakes; He has endowed each of us with unique gifts, making us priceless and invaluable. John Maxwell's wisdom reminds us to place a "10" on everyone's head, recognizing and honoring the intrinsic value of each person. If only my teachers had understood this concept when I was growing up.

Throughout my life's journey, I have always endeavored to see the best in people, for that is how God created me. Whether working with leaders worldwide, teachers, or counselors, I share my story to emphasize the importance of valuing others. We must resist the urge to see the negative first, for by recognizing and acknowledging their value, we can unleash remarkable transformations.

No one likes to be devalued, and when we make others feel valued, we unlock the full potential of their love and greatness. My life is a testament to this truth, as I, once devalued and dismissed, went on to achieve great things, including earning an executive MBA from Harvard in my early 50s, writing two multi-award-winning books, and now embarking on this journey of writing another. Yes, it's me— a person of value who values others.

Profound Main Point

The true essence of leadership lies in the ability to see the inherent value in every individual. By recognizing and appreciating their strengths and unique qualities, we create an environment where people can thrive and realize their full potential. In valuing others, we empower them to become their best selves.

Personalized Quote

"In the mirror of every soul, there is a priceless reflection waiting to be discovered. As a leader, your greatest gift is the ability to see the value in others and help them see it in themselves."

"Truly, truly, I say to you, unless one is born again, he cannot see the kingdom of God."

These words, spoken by Jesus in the book of John, hold a profound truth that extends beyond mere spiritual rebirth. They remind us of the transformative power of perception and the importance of seeing the best in others.

In today's world, where judgment and criticism often overshadow empathy and understanding, it is crucial to cultivate a mindset that allows us to recognize and appreciate the true value of each individual.

The Book of John emphasizes the significance of looking beyond appearances and recognizing the divine essence that resides within every person.

Jesus himself exemplified this principle as he interacted with individuals from all walks of life, embracing their uniqueness and offering them compassion and guidance. He saw the true value in others, regardless of their social status, background, or shortcomings. As leaders, we must strive to emulate this approach in our personal and professional lives.

In a society that often emphasizes achievements, accolades, and external appearances, it is easy to overlook the inherent worth of individuals who may not conform to societal norms or meet conventional expectations.

However, the book of John reminds us that true value lies not in outward accomplishments or material possessions but in the richness of one's character, the depth of compassion, and the authenticity of their spirit.

To truly see and focus on the true value of others, we must first challenge our own biases and preconceived notions. We must approach every encounter with an open mind and a willingness to understand and appreciate the unique gifts and perspectives that others bring to the table. This requires setting aside our own judgments and allowing ourselves to be curious about their stories, experiences, and aspirations.

As leaders, it is our responsibility to create an environment that nurtures the development of individuals'

By recognizing and celebrating the talents and strengths of our team members, we empower them to reach their full potential. As we see the true value in others, we can provide them with opportunities for growth, mentorship, and support, fostering an atmosphere of collaboration and trust.

Moreover, by acknowledging the inherent worth and potential in every individual, we create a ripple effect of positivity and encouragement.

When we see the best in others, we inspire them to see the best in themselves. We unlock their potential, enabling them to make meaningful contributions and achieve their goals.

In short, the book of John teaches us that seeing and focusing on the true value in others is not only an act of kindness but also a transformative force.

As leaders, we have the power to influence and shape the lives of those around us. By adopting a mindset rooted in empathy, understanding, and appreciation, we can unlock the hidden potential within individuals and create a world where everyone's God-given gifts are valued.

Therefore, let us make a conscious effort to see the true value in others. Let us seek to understand their stories, appreciate their unique perspectives, and celebrate their talents. Let us be leaders who uplift and empower, fostering an environment where every individual feels seen, heard, and valued. By doing so, we can create a society that thrives on diversity, compassion, and the recognition of the inherent worth within each and every one of us.

Chapter 5

Sharing Your Vision for Self, Themself, and in the Culture You Have Envisioned

My story

In the early 1980s, I embarked on the journey of opening my first salon. My mind was brimming with a vision that felt out of this world. Like many dreamers, I imagined a future that was larger than life. We all have these grand visions, whether it's hitting the lottery or achieving a wonderful life, but often, they remain confined to the realms of our minds.

Every step I took in those early days was guided by the thoughts swirling in my head. But how did that turn out, you might wonder? The truth is, we all have big dreams and profound thoughts, but if they don't make their way onto paper, they remain mere abstract ideas, never taking shape in the real world. It was a lesson I had to learn.

As I sought knowledge and understanding, I realized that putting a vision on paper was not only crucial but also the first step toward creating a culture that could support that vision. My upbringing had been steeped in Italian culture, even though it was never written down.

When my family moved to America, we carried forward much of our culture, blending it with the diverse tapestry of American culture. Over time, our vision and culture evolved, as all living things do. John understood the vision that Jesus had shared, the culture it encompassed, and the expectations set by God. This vision was not just spoken; it was written in the Old Testament and reaffirmed in the New Testament, aligning with the laws of the Old. However, the most profound change came with Jesus's sacrifice for our sins.

When I began to put my personal vision on paper, it became the foundation for creating a culture and a system that could support it.

This process led to a deeper understanding of the expectations within the company, and our team embraced the vision wholeheartedly. They weren't just investing in a dream; they were investing in a vision they believed in and wanted to support.

Don't get me wrong, dreaming in our minds is a beautiful and essential aspect of human nature. We can change our dreams in the blink of an eye. However, when it comes to faith or leading a company, having a written vision and culture is paramount. It provides the compass that keeps us on course even as we navigate the ever-changing waters of life.

Profound Main Point

In the journey from dreams to reality, the act of writing down our vision is the transformative bridge. It not only crystallizes our dreams but also paves the way for a culture that can breathe life into those dreams. Just as faith provides a guiding light in our spiritual lives, a written vision and culture serve as the guiding compass in the realm of leadership and business.

Personal Quote

"Dreams are born in the beauty of our minds, but it's on paper that they take their first breath and become real. In faith and leadership, a written vision and culture are the anchors that keep us steady, no matter how turbulent the seas of change may be." Quote Giulio Veglio

In the book of John, we find profound teachings that offer guidance and wisdom on various aspects of life. As we delve into John's teachings, we discover valuable insights that can be applied to our personal lives and our roles as leaders who influence others in today's world. Let us explore how we can effectively share our vision, drawing inspiration from John's teachings and incorporating his Biblical quotes.

The Vision for Self

John 14:6 states,

"Jesus said to him, 'I am the way, and the truth, and the life. No one comes to the Father except through me.'"

This verse reminds us that true vision and purpose in life are found in a personal relationship with Jesus. As leaders, we must prioritize our spiritual growth, seeking a deep understanding of our identity in Christ. By aligning ourselves with God's purpose, we can effectively share our vision with authenticity and conviction.

The Vision for Themself

John 13:34-35 says, "A new command I give you: Love one another. As I have loved you, so you must love one another. By this, everyone will know that you are my disciples if you love one another."

In this teaching, Jesus emphasizes the importance of love and compassion. As leaders, we must cultivate a vision that encompasses the well-being and growth of those we lead. By demonstrating love in our interactions, we create an environment where individuals can thrive and contribute their best. Our vision should extend beyond personal success to include the upliftment of others.

The Vision in the Culture You Have Envisioned

John 17:15-18 states, "My prayer is not that you take them out of the world but that you protect them from the evil one."

They are not of the world, even as I am not of it. Sanctify them by the truth; your word is truth. As you sent me into the world, I have sent them into the world." These verses remind us that, as leaders, we are called to make a positive impact on the culture around us.

Our vision should reflect a desire to bring godly values and principles into our professional spheres. By being a light in the darkness, we can influence the culture and create a transformative vision that aligns with God's truth.

As a leader, it is essential to share your vision effectively. Here are a few practical steps to consider:

1. **Clearly Define Your Vision:** Spend time reflecting on your vision, ensuring that it aligns with your personal values and God's truth. Clearly articulate the purpose and direction you envision for yourself and your team.

2. **Communicate with Passion:** Share your vision with enthusiasm and conviction. Your passion will inspire and motivate others, encouraging them to align themselves with the vision you present.

3. **Connect Emotionally:** Craft your message in a way that resonates with the emotions and aspirations of your audience. By appealing to their hearts, you can create a deeper connection and foster a sense of belonging to the shared vision.

Lead by Example

Embody the vision you promote. Consistently demonstrate the values and principles you advocate, allowing others to witness the transformative power of your vision through your actions.

John's teachings offer profound insights into sharing our vision for self, themself, and in the culture, we have envisioned. By anchoring our vision

Chapter 6
Serving with Consistency and Excellence

As I reflect on my journey, I am reminded of the importance of serving with unwavering consistency and uncompromising excellence. In a world that often tempts us to cut corners or settle for mediocrity, my experiences have shown me the profound impact of consistently striving for excellence in everything we do.

Throughout my career, I have had the privilege of serving in various capacities, from running my own business to mentoring others and leading teams. It became abundantly clear to me that consistency and excellence were not just optional traits; they were the cornerstones of success and leadership.

Consistency is the steady hand that guides us through both calm and turbulent waters. It means showing up day in and day out, delivering on promises, and being reliable in our actions. It is a trait that builds trust and fosters enduring relationships.

Just as Jesus consistently demonstrated love, compassion, and faith, we, too, must be unwavering in our commitment to serving others.

Excellence, on the other hand, is the pursuit of the highest standard in everything we do. It is the relentless drive to go above and beyond, to exceed expectations, and to continually improve.

Excellence is not a one-time achievement but a continuous journey of growth and refinement. Just as John and Jesus set the standard for unwavering faith and dedication, we must set our own standards of excellence in our endeavors.

In my own life, I have witnessed the transformative power of serving with consistency and excellence. It has allowed me to not only achieve personal and professional success but also to make a positive impact on the lives of others.

Whether it was providing exceptional service to my clients, mentoring aspiring leaders, or simply being there for my family, the commitment to consistency and excellence has been the guiding principle.

In a world that often values instant gratification and shortcuts, I urge you to embrace the path of serving with consistency and excellence. It may not always be the easiest road, but it is the one that leads to lasting fulfillment and leaves a legacy of impact.

Just as I have found purpose and meaning in this journey, I believe you, too, can discover the profound rewards of serving with unwavering dedication and relentless pursuit of excellence.

Main Point

Serving with consistency and excellence is the foundation of true leadership and lasting impact. It is a commitment to the unwavering dedication, reliability, and the pursuit of the highest standard in everything we do. Just as Jesus and John set the example for unwavering faith and dedication, we must set our own standards of excellence in our endeavors.

Personal Quote

"In the tapestry of leadership, consistency weaves the threads of trust, and excellence embroiders the fabric of impact. Embrace these virtues, and your legacy will shine brightly for generations to come."

In this fast-paced and ever-changing world, we live in, it has become increasingly challenging to serve and influence others consistently. Many individuals and leaders give their best effort initially but struggle to maintain that level of commitment and excellence over time.

However, the teachings found in the book of John offer timeless wisdom and guidance on how to serve not just once but consistently, both personally and professionally. By examining the principles outlined in John's writings, we can uncover valuable insights that will enable us to serve with authenticity, excellence, and unwavering commitment.

Serving with Authenticity and Purpose

John 13:15 states, "I have set you an example that you should do as I have done for you."

Jesus, the ultimate servant leader, demonstrated the importance of serving with authenticity and purpose. He consistently served others, not out of a desire for recognition or personal gain, but from a genuine love for humanity. To serve consistently, we must align our actions with our inner values and motives, ensuring that our service is an expression of our true selves rather than a mere façade.

Embracing a Servant's Heart

John 13:14 reminds us,

"Now that I, your Lord and Teacher, have washed your feet, you also should wash one another's feet."

True service stems from a humble and selfless heart. It involves prioritizing the needs of others above our own and willingly stepping into roles that may be perceived as menial or beneath us. By adopting a servant's heart, we cultivate a mindset of empathy, compassion, and a genuine desire to uplift and support those we serve.

Consistency through Perseverance

John 15:4 states, "Remain in me, as I also remain in you. No branch can bear fruit by itself; it must remain in the vine.

Consistent service requires perseverance and a steadfast commitment to our purpose. Just as a branch must remain connected to the vine to bear fruit, we must stay connected to our source of inspiration and strength.

Establishing daily habits such as prayer, meditation, and reflection can help us stay rooted in our values and maintain a consistent posture of service.

Leading by Example

John 13:34-35 emphasizes, "A new command I give you: Love one another. As I have loved you, so you must love one another."

By this, everyone will know that you are my disciples if you love one another." As leaders, our actions speak louder than words. To influence others professionally, we must consistently model the values and behaviors we expect from those we lead. By leading with love, integrity, and a commitment to service, we inspire others to follow suit and create a positive ripple effect within our organizations and communities.

Consistency in service is not a one-time achievement but an ongoing commitment. By embracing the teachings found in the book of John, we can develop a foundation for serving with authenticity, excellence, and unwavering commitment.

It begins with aligning our actions with our inner values and motives, adopting a servant's heart, persevering through challenges, and leading by example.

Let us remember that consistent service is not about wearing a mask to impress others momentarily but about genuinely caring for and uplifting those we serve. Only through unwavering dedication and a genuine heart can we leave a lasting impact and make a difference in the lives of others.

Chapter 7

Honoring Your Temple - Health, Self-Respect, and God's Perspective

In the tapestry of our lives, our physical bodies are the vessels through which we experience the world, and it is our solemn duty to honor and care for them. Throughout my journey, I have come to realize the profound importance of maintaining our health, both for ourselves and in the eyes of our Creator.

There was a time when I believed my body was indestructible, as if smoking, drugs, and excessive drinking couldn't harm me or wear me down. It was a reckless belief that led me down a perilous path. In 1986, reality hit hard, and I found myself having to start over - not just for my business and my life, but for myself.

I couldn't navigate this challenging journey alone. With the unwavering support of family and the grace of God's hand, I embarked on a path of renewal, not only for my physical body but for my soul. It was a profound awakening to the realization that our bodies are not merely vessels but sacred temples chosen by God for our souls to reside in during our earthly journey.

Honoring our bodies through healthy living, proper nutrition, and self-respect is not just a matter of physical well-being but also spiritual and emotional well-being. Just as we are called to be stewards of the Earth, we are called to be stewards of our own bodies.

In the eyes of God, our bodies are a gift, a divine creation deserving of love, care, and respect. Our choices, whether in matters of health, relationships, or self-respect, reflect our appreciation for this gift. We are called to treat ourselves with kindness and compassion, for when we do, we are better equipped to serve others and fulfill our purpose in this world.

I have learned that true health goes beyond the physical; it encompasses our mental and spiritual well-being as well. It is a holistic approach that acknowledges the interconnectedness of our mind, body, and soul.

By honoring our temple, we find not only physical vitality but also spiritual clarity and emotional strength to navigate life's challenges.

In other words, honoring our temple is a profound act of self-respect, reverence for God's creation, and a commitment to a fulfilling life journey. Through the trials and tribulations, I have come to understand that our bodies are not indestructible, but they are resilient and can be renewed with love, faith, and the grace of God's guiding hand.

Main Point

Honoring our physical bodies as temples is a sacred duty, not just for our physical health but for our spiritual and emotional well-being as well. Our bodies are divine creations deserving of love, care, and respect, reflecting our appreciation for the gift given to us by God. In nurturing our temple, we find vitality, clarity, and strength to navigate life's challenges.

Personal Quote

"In the temple of our bodies, God's grace is the cornerstone, and self-respect is the foundation. As we honor and care for our sacred temple, we become vessels of love, purpose, and divine guidance."

Honoring Your Temple – Nurturing Body, Mind, and Soul

In the book of John, we find profound teachings that emphasize the importance of honoring our temple—the sacred vessel comprising our body, mind, and soul. Recognizing the interconnectedness of these aspects is key to our personal well-being and our effectiveness as leaders of influence. By exploring the teachings of John, we can gain valuable insights into how to nurture ourselves holistically, aligning our personal and professional lives with the principles of self-care, growth, and spiritual nourishment.

Caring for Your Physical Temple

John 2:19 reminds us, "Destroy this temple, and I will raise it again in three days."

While Jesus was referring to His own body, we can draw a parallel to the importance of caring for our physical temple. Our bodies are gifts, and by treating them with respect, nourishing them with wholesome food, engaging in regular exercise, and prioritizing rest and relaxation, we can optimize our physical well-being. Honoring our bodies enables us to have the energy, vitality, and resilience needed to fulfill our personal and professional responsibilities.

Cultivating a Renewed Mind

John 8:32 states,

"Then you will know the truth, and the truth will set you free."

Our minds are powerful tools that shape our perceptions, attitudes, and actions. To honor our temple, we must cultivate a renewed mind. This involves nurturing positive thoughts, practicing mindfulness and self- reflection, and engaging in continuous learning and personal growth. By immersing ourselves in uplifting literature, seeking knowledge, and surrounding ourselves with positive influences, we create an environment conducive to personal development and mental well-being.

Nourishing Your Spiritual Soul

John 4:24 affirms, "God is spirit, and his worshipers must worship in the Spirit and in truth."

Our spiritual well-being is of utmost importance, as it forms the foundation of our inner strength, purpose, and connection to something greater than ourselves.

Honoring our temple involves nurturing our spiritual soul through practices such as prayer, meditation, and contemplation. These practices allow us to deepen our relationship with the divine, find solace in times of adversity, and align our actions with our core values.

Key Point

To honor our temple, we must care for our physical bodies, cultivate a renewed mind, and nourish our spiritual souls. By nurturing these interconnected aspects, we can achieve a harmonious balance that enhances our personal and professional lives, enabling us to lead with authenticity, compassion, and effectiveness.

Call to Action

1. Commit to a daily self-care routine that includes exercise, healthy eating, and sufficient rest.

2. Engage in regular mindfulness and reflection practices to cultivate a renewed mind.

3. Dedicate time each day for spiritual nourishment through prayer, meditation, or reading sacred texts.

4. Seek opportunities for personal growth and learning, both personally and professionally.

5. Encourage and support team members in their own journey of honoring their temple.

Exercise

Take a few moments each day to reflect on how you are honoring your temple. Ask yourself:

- How can I better care for my physical body?

- What steps can I take to cultivate a renewed mind?

- How can I deepen my spiritual connection?

- Are there any changes I need to make in my daily habits to align with my holistic well-being?

Chapter 8
Knowing Yourself

In the journey of life and leadership, there is perhaps no more crucial endeavor than the quest to truly know oneself. This chapter is a reflection on the profound importance of self-awareness and the transformative power it holds.

Throughout my own life, I've come to understand that knowing oneself is not a static destination but an ongoing exploration. It is a journey that requires introspection, reflection, and a willingness to confront both our strengths and our weaknesses.

The process of self-discovery is not always easy. It often involves delving into the depths of our past experiences, confronting our fears and insecurities, and challenging the beliefs and assumptions that have shaped us. It requires a level of vulnerability and honesty that can be uncomfortable but is ultimately liberating.

Knowing oneself is not about creating an idealized version of who we want to be; rather, it is about embracing our authentic selves with all our imperfections and quirks. It is about acknowledging our strengths and using them to serve others while also recognizing our limitations and working to improve upon them.

In leadership, self-awareness is the cornerstone of effective decision-making and interpersonal relationships. It allows us to understand our motivations, values, and biases, which in turn helps us lead with greater empathy and authenticity.

Through self-awareness, we gain clarity about our purpose and our unique contribution to the world. It guides us in aligning our actions with our values and empowers us to make choices that are in harmony with our true selves.

I've also learned that knowing oneself is not a solitary endeavor. It often involves seeking feedback and insights from trusted mentors, friends, and colleagues who can offer a different perspective on our strengths and weaknesses. It is through these external reflections that we can refine our self-awareness and continue to grow.

In conclusion, the journey of knowing oneself is a lifelong pursuit that holds the power to transform not only our own lives but also the lives of those we lead. It is a path of self-discovery, authenticity, and growth that enables us to navigate the complexities of life and leadership with wisdom and grace.

Main Point

Knowing oneself is a profound journey of self-discovery, authenticity, and growth. It requires introspection, vulnerability, and a willingness to embrace both strengths and weaknesses. Self-awareness empowers us to lead with empathy and authenticity, align our actions with our values, and make meaningful contributions to the world.

Personal Quote

"In the mirror of self-awareness, we find the truest reflection of our soul's journey. Embrace your authentic self, for it is the compass that guides you to a life of purpose, wisdom, and genuine leadership."

****

In the book of John, we find profound teachings that emphasize the importance of knowing oneself and others. John's wisdom reveals that how we perceive ourselves directly influences how we perceive and understand those around us. This chapter explores the relevance of this concept in our personal lives and as leaders who impact others professionally in today's world.

Understanding Self-Perception

John's teachings remind us that self-awareness is the key to understanding others. As we delve into our own thoughts, emotions, and beliefs, we gain valuable insights into our strengths, weaknesses, and motivations. Through introspection, we can identify our biases, prejudices, and preconceived notions, allowing us to approach others with empathy and open-mindedness.

The Mirror Effect

John's words echo the idea that how we see ourselves is reflected in how we perceive others. When we embrace self-acceptance and cultivate a positive self-image, we are more likely to extend the same grace and understanding to those around us.

Conversely, if we harbor self-doubt or judgment, we may project those feelings onto others, hindering our ability to truly know and connect with them.

Applying John's Teachings Personally

To apply John's teachings in our personal lives, we must embark on a journey of self-discovery. We can start by reflecting on our values, passions, and purpose. Engaging in practices such as journaling, meditation, or seeking guidance from mentors can help us gain clarity and deepen our self-awareness. As we grow in understanding ourselves, we become better equipped to understand and appreciate the uniqueness of others.

Influencing Others Professionally

As leaders, it is crucial to recognize the impact our self-perception has on those we lead. John's teachings encourage us to lead with humility, compassion, and authenticity.

By fostering an environment that values self-reflection and personal growth, we inspire our team members to embark on their own journeys of self-discovery. Through active listening, empathy, and constructive feedback, we create a space where individuals feel seen, heard, and understood.

Biblical Quotes from the Book of John:

John 13:34-35 - "A new command I give you: Love one another. As I have loved you, so you must love one another. By this, everyone will know that you are my disciples if you love one another."

John 8:32 - "Then you will know the truth, and the truth will set you free."

Call to Action

In conclusion, John's teachings remind us of the profound connection between knowing ourselves and knowing others. To never stop serving with excellence and staying consistent, we must commit to continuous self-reflection and growth. Here are some exercises to provoke thought and action in your personal and professional life:

1. **Daily Reflection:** Set aside time each day to reflect on your thoughts, emotions, and actions. Consider how they align with your values and how they may influence your perception of others.

2. **Seek Feedback:** Ask trusted friends, colleagues, or mentors for honest feedback about how you come across to others. Use their insights to gain a deeper understanding of your strengths and areas for improvement.

3. **Practice Empathy:** Put yourself in someone else's shoes and try to understand their perspective without judgment. Engage in active listening and ask open-ended questions to foster meaningful connections.

4. **Embrace Diversity:** Surround yourself with individuals from diverse backgrounds and perspectives. Engage in conversations that challenge your assumptions and broaden your understanding of the world.

Remember, the journey of self-discovery and understanding others is ongoing. By embracing these practices, we can cultivate a deeper sense of self-awareness, positively influence those around us, and lead with excellence.

Never stop seeking the truth, for it will set you free.

Note

The exercises provided are meant to provoke thought and action. Feel free to adapt them to your personal and professional context, ensuring they align with your values and goals.

Chapter 9

Creating Genuine Care for Those We Lead - Love as the Foundation of Leadership

My Story

In the tapestry of leadership, one thread stands out above all others: the thread of genuine care and love for those we lead. This chapter delves into the profound importance of love as the foundational element of leadership and the transformative power it holds.

Throughout my journey, I've come to understand that leadership is not solely about authority, strategy, or achieving objectives. It is, at its core, about people—the individuals who look to us for guidance, inspiration, and support. It is in this space that love finds its place as the bedrock of true leadership.

Love in leadership is not a mere sentiment; it is an intentional and selfless act of caring for the well-being, growth, and happiness of those we lead. It is a commitment to seeing the value in every individual and creating an environment where they can flourish.

Genuine care and love are expressed through empathy, active listening, and a deep understanding of the needs and aspirations of our team members. It means being there not only in times of success but also in times of struggle and vulnerability.

In the example of Jesus and his disciples, we see a profound demonstration of love as the cornerstone of leadership. Jesus didn't just instruct; he nurtured, guided, and deeply cared for his followers. His love transcended boundaries and transformed lives.

When we lead with love, we create a culture of trust, respect, and collaboration. It fosters a sense of belonging and inspires individuals to give their best. Love is the catalyst for growth, motivation, and the realization of human potential.

However, it's essential to note that love in leadership doesn't mean avoiding tough decisions or overlooking areas that require improvement. It means making those decisions with empathy and a genuine concern for the greater good of all.

In conclusion, genuine care and love for those we lead are not weaknesses but the greatest strengths of leadership. Love is the foundation upon which trust, growth, and meaningful relationships are built. It is the thread that weaves together the fabric of great leadership, leaving a lasting legacy of inspiration and positive impact.

Main Point

In the realm of leadership, genuine care and love for those we lead are the cornerstones of true success. Love is not a mere sentiment but an intentional act of empathy, understanding, and selfless commitment to the well-being and growth of others. It creates a culture of trust, respect, and collaboration, inspiring individuals to reach their fullest potential.

Personal Quote

"Love is the bedrock upon which great leadership is built. It is the thread that weaves the tapestry of trust, inspiration, and lasting impact. Lead with love, and you will nurture the hearts and minds of those you serve."

The Transformative Leadership Principles of John

In this chapter, we will explore the profound teachings of John, as recorded in the Bible, and how they can guide us in becoming influential and transformative leaders. We will delve into the ten bullet points that highlight the essence of John's teachings and discuss their application in both our personal and professional lives. By embracing these principles, we can lead with excellence, inspire others, and make a lasting impact in today's world.

Love and Compassion

John teaches us that love is the foundation of leadership. As leaders, we must cultivate genuine care for those we lead, showing compassion and empathy in our interactions. By leading with love, we create an environment where individuals feel valued, supported, and motivated to excel.

Quote: "A new command I give you: Love one another. As I have loved you, so you must love one another." - John 13:34

Servant Leadership

John emphasizes the importance of servant leadership, where leaders prioritize the needs of others above their own. By humbly serving those we lead, we inspire trust, foster collaboration, and create a culture of teamwork and unity.

Quote: "Whoever wants to become great among you must be your servant." - John 12:26

Integrity and Truth

John teaches us the significance of leading with integrity and truthfulness. As leaders, we must be honest, transparent, and consistent in our words and actions. By upholding these values, we build trust and credibility, which are essential for effective leadership.

Quote: "Then you will know the truth, and the truth will set you free." - John 8:32

Vision and Purpose

John encourages us to have a clear vision and purpose in our leadership. By setting meaningful goals and inspiring others with a compelling vision, we can motivate individuals to work towards a common objective, fostering growth and progress.

Quote: "I have come that they may have life and have it to the full." - John 10:10

Empowerment and Development

John teaches us to empower and develop those we lead. By investing in their growth, providing opportunities for learning and advancement, and nurturing their talents, we unlock their full potential and create a thriving and high-performing team.

Quote: "Very truly I tell you, whoever believes in me will do the works I have been doing, and they will do even greater things than these." - John 14:12

Resilience and Perseverance

John's teachings remind us of the importance of resilience and perseverance in leadership. Challenges and setbacks are inevitable, but by staying steadfast in our commitment and overcoming obstacles, we inspire others to do the same, fostering a culture of resilience and determination.

Quote: "In this world, you will have trouble. But take heart! I have overcome the world." - John 16:33

Humility and Teachability

John emphasizes the value of humility and a teachable spirit in leadership. By acknowledging that we don't have all the answers and remaining open to learning from others, we create an environment that encourages innovation, growth, and continuous improvement.

Quote: "I am the way and the truth and the life. No one comes to the Father except through me." - John 14:6

In conclusion, John's teachings provide us with timeless principles that can guide us in becoming influential and transformative leaders. By embracing love, servant leadership, integrity, vision, empowerment, resilience, humility, and teachability, we can lead with excellence and make a positive impact in our personal and professional lives.

Call to Action

Never stop serving with excellence and staying consistent; I encourage you to reflect on the following exercises:

1.   Reflect on your leadership style and identify areas where you can incorporate more love, compassion, and servant leadership.

2.   Set a clear vision and purpose for your personal and professional life, and regularly communicate it to inspire and motivate others.

3.   Seek opportunities to empower and develop those you lead, providing mentorship and support for their growth.

4.   Cultivate resilience and perseverance by embracing challenges as opportunities for growth and learning.

5.   Practice humility and remain teachable, seeking wisdom from others and being open to new ideas and perspectives.

By consistently applying these principles and engaging in these exercises, you will not only become a better leader but also inspire and transform those around you.

Chapter 10
The Power of Influence and Testimony Through Wisdom & Knowledge

Once upon a time, in a small village nestled amidst rolling hills, there lived a wise old man named Samuel. Samuel was known far and wide for his vast wisdom and knowledge. People from all walks of life would seek his counsel, hoping to gain insights and guidance for their problems.

Samuel firmly believed in the power of sharing wisdom and knowledge. He understood that knowledge was not meant to be hoarded but rather to be shared with others. He believed that by sharing what he knew, he could make a positive impact on the lives of those around him.

One day, a young woman named Emily approached Samuel with a heavy heart. She was facing a difficult decision and was unsure of what path to take. Samuel listened attentively to her concerns and then began to share his wisdom. He spoke of his own experiences, the lessons he had learned, and the insights he had gained over the years.

As Samuel shared his wisdom, Emily's face lit up with newfound clarity. She realized that by tapping into Samuel's knowledge, she could make a more informed decision. Samuel's guidance not only helped Emily in that moment but also empowered her to make wiser choices in the future.

The village thrived because of Samuel's willingness to share his wisdom. People would gather around him, eager to learn from his vast knowledge. Samuel would hold regular gatherings where he would impart his wisdom to anyone who sought it. The village became a hub of learning and growth, with individuals constantly seeking to expand their own knowledge.

Samuel understood that wisdom and knowledge were not finite resources. The more he shared, the more he seemed to receive in return. He believed that the pursuit of wisdom and knowledge should be a lifelong journey. He encouraged others to never stop learning, to remain curious, and to seek out new experiences.

As the years went by, Samuel grew older, but his thirst for knowledge remained unquenchable. He continued to learn from others, embracing new ideas and perspectives. Even in his old age, he remained a beacon of wisdom, guiding and inspiring those around him.

The importance of sharing wisdom and knowledge became evident to everyone in the village. It created a sense of unity and growth as individuals supported and uplifted one another. The village became a place where people thrived, not just because of Samuel's wisdom but because they, too, began to share their own knowledge with others.

In the end, Samuel's legacy was not just the wisdom he possessed but the ripple effect he created by sharing it. He taught the village that knowledge was a gift meant to be shared and that by doing so, they could collectively create a brighter and more enlightened community.

And so, the village continued to flourish, with each generation passing down the wisdom and knowledge they had acquired. They understood that the pursuit of wisdom was a lifelong journey and that by sharing it, they could help others navigate the complexities of life. For in the act of sharing wisdom, they discovered the true power of knowledge - its ability to transform lives and build a better world.

In the bustling city of modern times, where knowledge and wisdom are highly sought after, there lived a remarkable leader named Sarah. She was known for her exceptional ability to influence others both personally and professionally. Sarah's secret lay in her deep understanding of the teachings of John, a revered figure whose words held timeless wisdom.

As Sarah delved into the book of John, she discovered profound insights that resonated with her own journey of personal growth and leadership. She realized that to truly influence others, she needed to first embody the principles she wished to impart. John's teachings became her guiding light, illuminating her path toward becoming a more effective leader.

One of John's powerful quotes that deeply impacted Sarah was, "You will know the truth, and the truth will set you free." Sarah understood that seeking knowledge and truth was not merely an intellectual pursuit but a transformative journey. She encouraged those around her to embrace a mindset of continuous learning and growth, both personally and professionally.

Sarah recognized that her influence extended beyond her immediate circle. She understood that her actions and words had the power to inspire and motivate others in the wider world. She embraced her role as a leader with humility and a genuine desire to make a positive impact.

In her quest to influence others, Sarah developed a series of thought-provoking exercises that encouraged introspection and action. She encouraged individuals to reflect on their personal values and align them with their professional goals.

Through journaling and self-reflection, she guided them to identify areas of growth and develop strategies to overcome challenges.

Sarah's call to action was simple yet profound: never stop serving with excellence and stay consistent. She emphasized the importance of maintaining integrity and authenticity in all endeavors. She reminded her followers that true influence comes from a place of genuine care and empathy for others.

Sarah shared her personal testimony of how John's teachings had transformed her life. She encouraged her readers to explore the book of John themselves, to seek knowledge and wisdom, and to apply these timeless principles in their own lives.

In this chapter, we have explored the power of influence and testimony, drawing inspiration from the teachings of John. We have seen how these teachings can be applied personally and professionally in today's world. Now, it is time for you to embark on your own journey of influence and growth.

Exercise

Take a moment to reflect on your personal and professional life. Identify one area where you can make a positive impact and influence others. Develop a plan of action to implement this change, keeping in mind the principles of integrity, authenticity, and continuous learning. Remember, your influence has the potential to shape lives and create a ripple effect of positive change.

As you move forward, never stop serving with excellence and stay consistent in your pursuit of knowledge and wisdom. Embrace the teachings of John and let them guide you on your path to becoming a truly influential leader.

May your journey be filled with purpose, growth, and the unwavering desire to make a difference in the lives of others.

In the grand tapestry of leadership, there is no force more potent than the power of influence, driven by wisdom and knowledge. This chapter explores the profound impact John's seeking of wisdom and knowledge has on our ability to lead and inspire others.

Throughout my journey, I've come to understand that the pursuit of wisdom and knowledge is not a destination but a lifelong journey. It is a path paved with both successes and failures, a continuous quest to deepen our understanding of the world and the people within it.

As a leader, my ability to influence others has always been intimately tied to my willingness to seek out wisdom and knowledge. It is through this relentless pursuit that I have been able to navigate the complexities of leadership, make informed decisions, and inspire those around me.

One of the most vital lessons I've learned is that the moment we think we know it all is the moment we start to fall. The humility to acknowledge that there is always more to learn is a hallmark of great leadership. It is a reminder that wisdom and knowledge are vast oceans, and we are but humble vessels ever in need of filling.

Writing this book is a testament to the ongoing journey of seeking wisdom and knowledge. The process of research, learning, and refining my writing skills has deepened my understanding of leadership. It is a reminder that our capacity to influence and share wisdom is inexhaustible so long as we remain committed to learning and growing.

In the example set by Jesus and his disciples, we see the embodiment of this philosophy. Jesus, despite his divinity, was a lifelong learner and a relentless seeker of wisdom. His influence over others like John was not solely due to his inherent wisdom but also his ability to share and impart that wisdom in ways that resonated deeply.

As leaders, we must recognize that our journey of learning and influence is not for our own sake but for the betterment of those we lead. By continuously seeking wisdom and knowledge, we enrich our ability to inspire, guide, and uplift others on their own journeys.

The power of influence through wisdom and knowledge is a journey without end. It is a testament to our commitment to growth, our capacity to inspire, and our dedication to serving others. As long as we continue to seek, learn, influence, and share, our legacy as leaders will endure long after we are gone.

Main Point

The power of influence through wisdom and knowledge is a lifelong journey that defines great leadership. It is a reminder that we are perpetual learners, ever seeking to deepen our understanding and enrich our capacity to inspire and guide others. The day we stop learning and influencing is the day our journey as leaders truly ends.

"In the pages of wisdom and the chapters of knowledge, we find the ink with which we write our legacy of influence. The pursuit of wisdom is the eternal flame that lights the path of leadership." Giulio Veglio.

Chapter 11
Modeling the Process

In the intricate tapestry of leadership, there is a fundamental truth that cannot be ignored: people do what people see. This chapter explores the profound impact of leading by example and the responsibility it places upon us as leaders.

I vividly recall a moment when I found myself perplexed by the behavior of some of my co-workers on the management team. They were openly displaying their frustration, raising their voices, and treating our team members with disrespect. It was a troubling sight, and I called them into my office to address their behavior. As I spoke passionately about the importance of treating others with kindness and respect, a realization dawned upon me—an epiphany that changed my perspective forever.

I recognized that they were not acting out of nowhere; they were emulating my own behavior. It was a powerful moment of self-awareness. I understood that how I led was how they would lead, and the influence I exerted was far-reaching, creating a trickle-down effect throughout the organization.

Initially, I tried to rationalize my actions, telling myself that I wasn't yelling at them but merely expressing my frustrations, hoping they would convey my message with more tact. However, this rationalization was flawed. I should have never assumed that my intentions were clear, and I should have realized that expressing myself in such a manner was never the right approach.

This epiphany transformed my leadership style. I embraced the notion that leaders must lead by example, demonstrating the behaviors and values they wish to see in their teams. It became clear that the behaviors and culture within an organization often mirror the actions and attitudes of its top leaders.

In my work as a consultant, I've observed time and again that issues within companies—whether they involve communication breakdowns, a hostile environment, or rampant gossip—can often be traced back to the behavior of the top leader within that department or organization.

As leaders, we must recognize the tremendous influence we have over our teams. We set the tone, establish the culture, and shape the organization's values through our actions and behaviors. It is not enough to tell others what to do; we must show them by example.

In conclusion, modeling the process is not just a leadership principle; it is a responsibility. We must lead with integrity, empathy, and respect, for our actions speak louder than our words. By leading by example, we create a culture of accountability, inspiration, and positive change that ripples throughout our organizations and beyond.

Main Point

Modeling the process is not just a leadership choice; it is a profound responsibility. As leaders, we must recognize that our actions and behaviors set the tone for our teams and organizations. Leading by example, with integrity, empathy, and respect, creates a culture of accountability and positive change.

Personal Quote

"In the mirror of our actions, our teams see not just what we say but who we are. Leadership is not about telling others what to do; it's about showing them how to do it—with integrity, empathy, and respect."

Let's visit how John lead by example:

John, one of the twelve apostles of Jesus Christ, was a keen observer and a faithful follower. He was often referred to as "the disciple whom Jesus loved," and his close relationship with Jesus allowed him to absorb and model the teachings of Jesus in a profound way.

In the Gospel of John, we see John modeling Jesus' teachings through his actions and words. One of the most significant teachings of Jesus that John modeled was the commandment of love. In John 13:34-35, Jesus says,

"A new command I give you: Love one another. As I have loved you, so you must love one another. By this, everyone will know that you are my disciples if you love one another."

John took this teaching to heart and modeled it in his life. He was known for his deep love for the Christian community and his commitment to spreading the message of love. In his first epistle, John 4:7-8, he wrote,

"Beloved, let us love one another, for love is from God, and whoever loves has been born of God and knows God. Anyone who does not love does not know God, because God is love."

Another teaching of Jesus that John modeled was the importance of faith. In John 20:29, Jesus says,

"Because you have seen me, you have believed; blessed are those who have not seen and yet have believed."

John demonstrated his faith by believing in Jesus even when he was not physically present. He encouraged others to do the same, writing in John 5:4,

"For everyone born of God overcomes the world. This is the victory that has overcome the world, even our faith."

Through his life and writings, John modeled the teachings of Jesus, emphasizing the importance of love and faith. He served as a living example of what it means to be a disciple of Jesus, embodying the teachings he had received and passing them on to others.

Let me share the story of a man called Ethan, who had a unique way of modeling processes. He believed in the power of love, integrity, and honesty, and he incorporated these values into his models. There is a saying he lived by and heard,

"People do what people see," and Ethan made sure his actions reflected his beliefs.

One day, Ethan met a young man named Peter. Peter was struggling with his life, unable to find a direction. Ethan decided to help Peter by modeling the process of love, integrity, and honesty. He started by showing Peter the importance of love.,

"Love is not just a feeling; it's a decision. It's about putting others before yourself."

This was a quote from Mother Teresa, a famous humanitarian.

Next, Ethan modeled integrity.

"Integrity is doing the right thing, even when no one is watching."

This quote is from C.S. Lewis, a renowned author, perfectly encapsulated John's belief in integrity.

Finally, Ethan demonstrated honesty.

"Honesty is the best policy. If I lose my honor, I lose myself." quoted Mark Twain,

Ethan lived by this, always being truthful and transparent in his actions.

Ethan also incorporated biblical quotes from the book of John into his teachings. He often quoted John 13:34,

"A new command I give you: Love one another. As I have loved you, so you must love one another."

He believed this verse embodied the essence of love, integrity, and honesty.

Call to Action

Ethan's way of modeling processes is a testament to the power of love, integrity, and honesty through the teaching of the Book of John and his examples of Modeling the Process. It's a call to action for us to incorporate these values into our lives. As Ethan and John did, we should strive to model these values in our actions, for as people do what people see.

Modeling the process as Ethan or John did is not easy, but it's worth it. It requires a commitment to love, integrity, and honesty. But remember, as John often said,

"The journey of a thousand miles begins with a single step."

Exercises

1. Reflect on your actions. Are they in line with the values of love, integrity, and honesty?

2. Practice empathy. Try to understand others' perspectives and respond with love.

3. Be accountable. If you make a mistake, own up to it. This is a true demonstration of integrity.

4. Be honest with yourself. Identify areas in your life where you can improve and make a commitment to do so.

Remember, the goal is not to be perfect but to be better than you were yesterday. As you model the process for others, you'll find that you're also modeling it for yourself.

Chapter 12
Never Thirst Again

The quest for wisdom and knowledge is a lifelong journey, a thirst that is never fully quenched. This concept is deeply rooted in the teachings of the Bible, particularly in the book of John. In John 4:14, Jesus says, "Whoever drinks the water I give them will never thirst. Indeed, the water I give them will become in them a spring of water welling up to eternal life.

"This verse is not about physical thirst but a metaphorical thirst for wisdom and knowledge."

In the story of Jesus and the Samaritan woman at the well, Jesus offers her 'living water,' a symbol of the wisdom and knowledge that leads to eternal life. The woman, initially thinking in literal terms, is confused.

But Jesus explains that the water he offers is spiritual, satisfying the soul's thirst for truth and understanding.

In today's world, we can interpret this as a call to continually seek wisdom and knowledge, both personally and professionally. As Albert Einstein once said,

"Wisdom is not a product of schooling but of the lifelong attempt to acquire it."

This thirst for wisdom and knowledge should be our driving force, pushing us to learn, grow, and evolve.

In our personal lives, this could mean seeking to understand ourselves better, learning from our mistakes, and striving to be better individuals. Professionally, it could mean continually updating our skills, staying abreast of industry trends, and seeking innovative solutions.

The thirst for wisdom and knowledge is not a one-time event but a continuous process. As Benjamin Franklin said,

"An investment in knowledge pays the best interest."

We must continually invest in our knowledge and wisdom to stay 'hydrated.

The quest for wisdom and knowledge is a journey that never ends. Like the Samaritan woman at the well, we must seek the 'living water' that Jesus offers - the wisdom and knowledge that satisfies our soul's thirst. As we navigate through life, let us remember the words of Socrates and continue to thirst for wisdom and knowledge.

"The only true wisdom is in knowing you know nothing,"

Exercises

1. Set aside time each day for learning. This could be reading a book, listening to a podcast, or taking an online course.

2. Practice mindfulness. This helps us to be present in the moment and opens us up to new insights and wisdom.

3. Engage in discussions and debates. This helps to broaden our perspectives and deepen our understanding.

4. Keep a journal. Reflecting on our experiences can provide valuable insights and wisdom.

5. Seek mentorship. Learning from those who have walked the path before us can provide invaluable knowledge and wisdom.

Remember, the key to never thirsting again is to continually seek wisdom and knowledge. As we quench our thirst, we become wellsprings of wisdom overflowing with knowledge and understanding, ready to share with the world.

Chapter 13
Feeding Others
Nourishing Minds and Souls

In this chapter of life and leadership, there is a profound lesson to be found in the act of nourishing minds and feeding the souls of those we encounter. This chapter dives into the transformative power of feeding others with purpose and intention.

In the Book of John, we find the inspiring story of how Jesus fed his people, not just with physical sustenance but with profound spiritual nourishment. It is a story that resonates deeply with me, as it reminds me of a pivotal moment in my own journey.

Many years ago, when I was just starting my career as a teacher and speaker, I had the privilege of meeting a remarkable woman named Kitty Victor. She was a fellow teacher and speaker, a globetrotter who had written books and interviewed countless great leaders in her time—a true luminary. It was during our meeting that she felt compelled to gift me a Bible.

As I accepted this thoughtful gift and opened it, I turned to a page that told the story of how Jesus fed his people. It was a moment that felt divinely orchestrated. In that instant, I received a profound message from the divine—a message that would forever change my perspective on teaching and speaking.

I realized that it was not about me; it was not about how I looked or sounded on stage, nor was it about feeding my own ego. It was about the people I stood before, the individuals I had the privilege to teach and speak to. What mattered most was what I could give them—information, knowledge, and inspiration that would transform their lives and help them achieve their dreams.

In that sacred moment, a weight was lifted from my shoulders. The anxiety and stress I used to feel before stepping onto the stage began to dissipate. I discovered my true purpose—to feed the minds and souls of those I had the honor to serve. This newfound clarity propelled me forward, leading to more teaching and speaking engagements, not only in the United States but in various countries, colleges, and esteemed national and international organizations.

This profound lesson also deeply influenced how I led my teams in my own businesses. I understood that leadership was not merely about authority; it was about guiding, inspiring, and nurturing the growth of those under my care. Just as Jesus nourished his people, I sought to nourish the minds and spirits of my team members.

In conclusion, the act of feeding others with purpose is a testament to our commitment to making a positive impact on the lives of those we encounter. It is a reminder that leadership is not about us but about the profound difference we can make in the lives of others. It is a journey of purpose, intention, and transformation that leaves a lasting legacy of inspiration and empowerment.

Main Point

Nourishing minds and feeding the souls of others is a profound act of purpose-driven leadership. It is a reminder that leadership is not about us but about the profound difference we can make in the lives of others. Just as Jesus fed his people, we have the power to nourish minds and spirits, leaving a lasting legacy of inspiration and empowerment.

Personal Quote

"In the banquet of leadership, the most nourishing feast is the one we serve to others. Purpose-driven leadership is not about us; it's about the profound difference we can make in the lives of those we serve." Giulio Veglio

****

In the book of John in the Bible, there is a profound message about the importance of feeding others, not just with physical sustenance but also with lessons and thoughts that elevate and inspire. This concept holds relevance in both our personal and professional lives, as it guides us to be leaders who nourish ourselves and those around us.

In John 6:35, Jesus declares,

"I am the bread of life. Whoever comes to me will never go hungry, and whoever believes in me will never be thirsty."

This statement goes beyond the literal meaning of physical hunger and thirst. It emphasizes the spiritual hunger and thirst that exist within each of us. Just as we need food and water to sustain our bodies, we also require knowledge, wisdom, and inspiration to nourish our minds and souls.

To truly feed others, we must first feed ourselves. We need to continuously seek wisdom and knowledge, both from the scriptures and from various sources of inspiration. As we grow personally and professionally, we accumulate a wealth of insights and experiences that can be shared with others. This sharing becomes a form of nourishment as we provide guidance, support, and encouragement to those around us.

One biblical story from the book of John that exemplifies the concept of feeding others is the miracle of the feeding of the five thousand (John 6:1-15). In this story, Jesus takes five loaves of bread and two fish, blesses them, and miraculously multiplies them to feed a multitude of people. This miracle not only satisfies their physical hunger but also demonstrates the power of abundance and the importance of sharing.

In addition to biblical teachings, there are numerous quotes from famous individuals that reinforce the significance of feeding others. Mahatma Gandhi once said,

"The best way to find yourself is to lose yourself in the service of others."

This quote reminds us that by selflessly serving and nourishing others, we discover our own purpose and fulfillment.

The act of feeding others goes beyond providing physical sustenance. It involves nourishing minds and souls with lessons, thoughts, and inspiration. By drawing from the teachings in the book of John and other scriptures, we can find guidance on how to inspire and uplift others in today's world.

Personally, we must continuously seek wisdom and knowledge to share with those around us. Professionally, we can lead by example, fostering an environment of growth and support. As we strive to keep ourselves well-hydrated with wisdom and knowledge, we can extend the same nourishment to others, creating a ripple effect of positive change and transformation.

The Five Exercises of Serving and Feeding Others

Once upon a time, in a small town named Hammondville lived a wise old man named Elijah. He was known for his wisdom and leadership, and he believed in feeding others not just physically but also spiritually and intellectually. He devised five exercises that he believed could help anyone become a better servant and leader.

The Exercise of Empathy

Elijah believed that to truly serve others, one must first understand them. He encouraged everyone to spend a day in the shoes of another person. This exercise was not just about understanding their physical needs but also their emotional and spiritual needs. It taught the townsfolk to be more compassionate and understanding, which in turn made them better leaders.

The Exercise of Sharing Knowledge

Elijah was a firm believer in the power of education. He set up a weekly gathering where everyone in the town could share something they had learned. This exercise fed the minds of the townsfolk, keeping them intellectually stimulated and always eager to learn more.

The Exercise of Mindful Listening

Elijah taught the townsfolk the importance of truly listening to others. He believed that by listening mindfully, one could understand the unspoken needs and desires of others. This exercise helped the townsfolk become more attuned to each other's needs, making them better at serving and leading.

The Exercise of Selfless Service

Elijah encouraged the townsfolk to spend one day a week serving others without expecting anything in return. This could be anything from helping a neighbor with their chores to volunteering at the local shelter. This exercise taught the townsfolk the joy of giving and the importance of selflessness in leadership.

The Exercise of Reflection

Lastly, Elijah believed in the power of reflection. He encouraged the townsfolk to spend some time each day reflecting on their actions and how they could improve. This exercise helped the townsfolk become more self-aware and strive for continuous improvement, both crucial qualities in a leader.

These exercises transformed Harmonyville. The townsfolk became more compassionate, understanding, and selfless. They became better at serving others and leading. And most importantly, they learned the importance of feeding others not just physically but also spiritually and intellectually. They learned that by doing so, they could keep their community full until it was time to eat again.

Chapter 14

The Art of Connection
Lessons from John

In the Biblical book of John, we find a wealth of wisdom on how to communicate and connect with others. John, one of Jesus' closest disciples, was not just a communicator; he was a connector. He had a unique ability to reach people's hearts and minds, transcending the barriers of language, culture, and social status.

One of the most poignant stories that illustrate John's connection with others is the account of Jesus washing the disciples' feet (John 13:1-17). John, witnessing this act of humility and service, was deeply moved. He understood that Jesus was not merely performing a menial task, but also demonstrating a profound lesson in leadership and connection.

John quotes Jesus saying,

"A new command I give you: Love one another. As I have loved you, so you must love one another." (John 13:34)

This commandment is not just about expressing affection; it's about understanding, empathy, and connection. It's about putting others' needs before our own, just as Jesus did.

In today's world, leaders can learn from John's teachings. In a society often divided by differences, we need leaders who can connect, who can wash the feet of their followers in a metaphorical sense. Leaders like Nelson Mandela, who once said,

"If you want to make peace with your enemy, you have to work with your enemy. Then he becomes your partner."

This echoes John's teachings of love and connection.

As leaders, we must strive to understand those we lead, empathize with their struggles, and serve their needs. This is the essence of connection, and it's a powerful tool for change.

John's teachings remind us that true connection goes beyond mere communication. It requires empathy, understanding, and a willingness to serve. As leaders, let's strive to embody these qualities, fostering a culture of connection in our personal and professional lives.

Call to Action

Let's take a moment to reflect on our leadership style. Are we merely communicating, or are we truly connecting? Let's strive to be leaders who connect, following the example set by John and Jesus.

Exercises

1. Reflect on a time when you felt truly connected to someone. What made that connection so strong? How can you foster similar connections in your leadership role?
2. Identify a person in your professional life with whom you struggle to connect. What steps can you take to understand and empathize with them better?
3. Consider the concept of servant leadership. How can you serve those you lead in a way that fosters connection?
4. Reflect on John 13:34. How can you show love to those you lead.

5.   Identify a leader you admire for their ability to connect with others. What qualities do they possess that you can emulate in your leadership style?

Chapter 15

Leadership Beyond Titles: The Evolution of Leadership

In the intricate tapestry of leadership, there has been a profound evolution in the significance of titles and the essence of true leadership. This chapter explores the changing landscape of leadership, where titles have shifted from symbols of earned recognition to potential markers of entitlement.

In bygone eras, a title held deep significance. It was a badge of honor, a well-earned promotion bestowed upon those who demonstrated dedication, commitment, purpose, and exemplary leadership. People wore their titles with pride and commanded respect through their actions and character.

Throughout my journey, my focus was always on doing what was asked of me and what was best for all, infused with integrity and hard work. My aim was to help and empower others to achieve remarkable possibilities, all while upholding the culture and systems that enabled others to learn and understand. My leadership was driven by purpose, love, and genuine intentions.

I vividly recall the surprise and honor I felt when entrusted with leadership roles and titles. However, I never viewed these promotions as positions of empowerment; rather, they were recognitions of the hard work and dedication I had invested in all I did. I held these titles with pride and unwaveringly maintained my commitment to leadership.

Today, the meaning of titles has undergone a significant transformation. For many, titles have become symbols of entitlement, a declaration of "I want it now" rather than a testament to dedication and hard work. This shift has brought about a change in the essence of leadership.

In my own businesses, I made the deliberate decision to move away from the traditional model of titles and instead introduced postings of creative masters who led and empowered their teams. I reimagined office spaces to limit individual offices, promoting a culture where leaders were present and hands-on with their team members.

A leader's role, in my belief, is to ensure that every team member is equipped with the tools and training they need to be effective and productive. Moreover, leaders should be actively engaged in training and mentoring individuals to replace themselves—a practice that ensures continuous growth and succession planning.

I hold steadfast to the belief that titles are not mere decorations to be handed out indiscriminately but are earned through dedication, commitment, and exemplary leadership. True leaders are defined by their actions, their ability to inspire and empower others, and their unwavering commitment to the growth and success of their teams.

In conclusion, leadership beyond titles is a reflection of the evolving landscape of leadership, where true leaders rise above entitlement and embrace the essence of genuine leadership. It is a commitment to leading by example, empowering others, and continually earning the respect and trust of those we serve.

Main Point

Leadership beyond titles signifies a shift in the meaning of leadership, where titles are no longer symbols of entitlement but markers of dedication and exemplary leadership. True leaders rise above entitlement, lead by example, empower others, and continually earn respect and trust.

Personal Quote

"In the ever-evolving tapestry of leadership, titles are not entitlements but acknowledgments of dedication and commitment. True leadership is defined by actions, not titles."

****

John, a humble fisherman, was not born into a position of power or prestige. Yet, he was chosen by Jesus to be one of his twelve apostles, a testament to the fact that leadership is not about titles, but about character, actions, and influence.

In the book of John, we see numerous instances where leadership is demonstrated without the need for a formal title. Jesus himself, though he was the Son of God, did not claim a worldly title. Instead, he led through his actions, teachings, and love for humanity.

John 13:14-15 says,

"If I then, your Lord and Teacher, have washed your feet, you also ought to wash one another's feet. For I have given you an example, that you also should do just as I have done to you."

This passage illustrates that true leadership is about service, humility, and setting an example for others to follow.

In today's world, where entitlement is often mistaken for leadership, we must remember that a title does not make a leader. Leadership is earned through trust, respect, and the ability to inspire and motivate others.

As John Quincy Adams once said,

"If your actions inspire others to dream more, learn more, do more and become more, you are a leader."

Applying this to our personal and professional lives, we can all be leaders in our own right. We can lead by example, by serving others, by standing up for what is right, and by inspiring those around us. We don't need a title to do that.

Leadership is not about titles or entitlement. It's about actions, influence, and the ability to inspire and motivate others. It's about being a servant first and a leader second.

Call to Action

1. Reflect on your actions. Are you inspiring others to be better?
2. Serve others. Look for opportunities to help and support those around you.
3. Stand up for what is right, even when it's difficult.
4. Be a positive influence. Your actions and words have the power to impact others.
5. Remember, leadership is not about titles. It's about character, actions, and influence.

Exercises

1. Identify a situation where you demonstrated leadership without having a formal title. How did it make you feel?

2. Reflect on a leader you admire who leads without a title. What qualities do they possess that you can emulate?

3. Write down three ways you can serve others in your personal and professional life.

4. Identify a situation where you stood up for what is right. How did it impact those around you?

5. Write down three actions you can take to be a positive influence in your personal and professional life.

Chapter 16
Credibility Through Results
A Lesson from John

In the intricate tapestry of leadership, there is an enduring truth that transcends words and rhetoric: credibility is forged through tangible results. This chapter explores the profound significance of actions over words and the vital role they play in establishing trust and credibility.

I firmly believe that actions speak louder than words. Throughout my journey, I have encountered individuals who excel in the art of self-promotion, tirelessly proclaiming their greatness and their ability to outperform others. They boast of their capabilities, confidently asserting their qualifications and readiness for the job at hand.

Yet, time and again, I have witnessed a stark disconnect between their words and their actions. When I sought evidence of their accomplishments or observed their behavior, it often failed to align with the grandiose claims they made. Their actions and knowledge fell short of their proclamations, leaving me with a sense of skepticism.

In my role as an interviewer or when individuals seek promotions, I have adopted a simple but powerful mantra: "Show me." I have come to realize that anyone can talk a big game, but the true test of credibility lies in one's ability to deliver tangible results.

I look for individuals who not only articulate their strengths but can also demonstrate them through their past achievements and their actions in the present. It is not enough to claim greatness; one must exhibit it consistently.

Credibility through results is not just about delivering on promises; it is about consistently showcasing one's competence, integrity, and commitment. It is a reflection of a leader's ability to translate words into meaningful actions that drive positive outcomes.

Actions that align with words foster trust and confidence among team members and colleagues. They create a sense of reliability, where individuals know that what is promised will be delivered. Such credibility is an invaluable asset in leadership, as it inspires others to follow and collaborate willingly.

In conclusion, credibility through results is a testament to the transformative power of action over words. It is a reminder that in the world of leadership, true credibility is earned through consistent, meaningful actions that align with one's claims. It is a beacon that guides us toward authentic leadership based on trust and credibility.

Main Point:

Credibility in leadership is built upon the foundation of tangible results and actions that align with words. Actions, not empty rhetoric, establish trust and reliability, inspiring others to follow and collaborate willingly.

Personal Quote:

"In the symphony of leadership, actions are the notes that compose the melody of credibility. Talk is cheap; it's the consistent, meaningful actions that resonate and inspire trust."

Jesus and John, the disciples and leaders of great faith, embodied this principle with unwavering conviction. They did not merely proclaim their beliefs; they lived them through their actions.

Throughout the Gospels, we see Jesus and John tirelessly ministering to the sick, comforting the downtrodden, and teaching profound lessons through their deeds. Their actions were a testament to their unwavering faith and the authenticity of their message.

When Jesus declared that he came to "seek and save the lost," his actions aligned with this proclamation, he sought out the marginalized, the outcasts, and the sinners, offering them love, forgiveness, and a path to redemption. His actions reinforced his words, and his credibility as a leader grew.

Similarly, John, the beloved disciple, was not merely a listener but a doer of the Word. His actions spoke volumes as he spread the message of love, faith, and salvation. His commitment to living out the teachings of Jesus exemplified the principle that actions carry greater weight than words alone.

In our own leadership journeys, we can draw inspiration from the profound example set by Jesus and John.

In the Bible, the book of John provides a profound example of credibility through results. John the Baptist was not just a man of words but a man of action. His credibility was not built on empty promises or grandiose speeches but on the tangible results of his actions.

One of the most striking examples of this is found in John 1:23, where John the Baptist says,

"I am the voice of one calling in the wilderness, 'Make straight the way for the Lord.'"

John did not merely speak these words, he lived them. He dedicated his life to preparing the way for Jesus, and his actions bore fruit when Jesus began his ministry.

This principle of credibility through results is not just applicable to biblical figures, but to us in our personal and professional lives as well. As leaders, our credibility is not built on what we say but on what we do. Our actions speak louder than our words, and it is through our actions that we build trust and credibility.

Consider the words of former U.S. President Theodore Roosevelt, who said,

"The most important single ingredient in the formula of success is knowing how to get along with people."

This quote underscores the importance of building relationships and delivering results, not just talking about them.

Credibility comes from results. It is not enough to talk a big game; we must also walk the walk. As leaders, we must strive to emulate John the Baptist, who built his credibility through his actions, not his words.

Call to Action

1. **Reflect on your actions:** Are they in line with your words? Are you delivering on your promises?
2. **Consider your results:** Are they building your credibility? Are they helping you build trust with others?

3. **Think about your leadership style:** Are you leading by example? Are you delivering results?

Exercises

1. Identify one area in your personal or professional life where your actions and words are not aligned. What steps can you take to align them?
2. Reflect on a time when you delivered on a promise. How did it impact your credibility?
3. Think about a leader you admire. What actions do they take that build their credibility?
4. Identify one action you can take today to improve your credibility.
5. Reflect on your results. Are they helping you build credibility? If not, what changes can you make?

"Credibility is not built on empty words, but on the foundation of actions that speak volumes." - Giulio Veglio

Chapter 17
The Art of Not Passing Judgment

Life and leadership, the act of passing judgment is a pervasive human inclination. Yet, this chapter explores the profound wisdom of reserving judgment for the Divine, for there is only one true Judge—God.

Throughout my journey, I have witnessed how easy it is for individuals to pass judgment, both in their personal lives and within their professional spheres. However, I hold the firm belief that the authority to pass judgment belongs solely to God, not to any human being.

During my younger years, I experienced firsthand the pain of being misjudged and cast aside by others. It was deeply disheartening to realize that people were quick to make assumptions and spread rumors without truly knowing me or making an effort to understand my truth. I grappled with the question of why some would want to propagate falsehoods and subject me to unwarranted judgment.

As the years unfolded, I came to understand that such behavior often stemmed from envy, jealousy, or the desire to participate in gossip. I came to a profound realization: I knew my own identity and truth, as did those who truly knew me. I had been focusing on the wrong people and the wrong things.

The lives of Jesus and John serve as powerful examples of individuals who were constantly subjected to judgment. However, this did not deter them from remaining true to themselves—loving, faithful, caring, and deeply committed to the mission of fulfilling God's will.

In my own journey, I have made a conscious choice never to pass judgment, recognizing that only God possesses the divine authority to do so. My opinions are formed based on what I genuinely know, not on hearsay or baseless assumptions. I understand that people may have a past, just as I did, and that it is not indicative of who they are today. This principle applies to all, and I extend grace and understanding to others as I hope they would to me.

I vividly recall an encounter with a friend who cast judgment on a man he perceived as homeless and a freeloader. However, I recognized the man and engaged him in conversation. To my friend's surprise, we learned that this man had become a wealthy philanthropist, actively involved in charitable projects, and dedicated to helping those in need. My friend's judgment swiftly transformed into admiration, and he vowed never to judge another person without knowing their story.

This experience reinforced the belief that everyone possesses a unique story, one that we may never fully comprehend. Passing judgment on others is a practice best left to the Divine, for we are all imperfect beings striving to navigate our own journeys.

In conclusion, the art of not passing judgment is a reminder that there is only one true Judge, and it is not us. It is a call to reserve judgment, extend understanding, and acknowledge that every person carries a story that we may never fully grasp. Who are we to pass judgment on others?

Main Point:

The art of not passing judgment reminds us that the authority to judge belongs to the Divine, not to us. It calls us to extend understanding, for every person carries a unique story that we may never fully comprehend.

Personal Quote:

"We are but imperfect weavers of stories. The art of not passing judgment is a call to reserve judgment for the Divine and extend understanding to those whose stories we may never fully know."

In the biblical book of John, we find a profound lesson on the importance of not passing judgment on others. John, a disciple of Jesus, was a man who lived his life by this principle. He was a witness to Jesus' teachings and actions, which were rooted in love, understanding, and acceptance.

One of the most powerful examples of this is found in John 8:7, where Jesus says,

"He that is without sin among you, let him first cast a stone at her."

This was in response to the Pharisees who were quick to judge and condemn a woman caught in adultery. Jesus, instead of passing judgment, offered forgiveness and urged the woman to sin no more.

In our personal and professional lives, it is crucial to refrain from passing judgment on others. This is because judgment often stems from a place of ignorance, misunderstanding, or prejudice. It creates a barrier that prevents us from understanding and empathizing with others.

Great leaders understand this principle. They know that to lead effectively, they must first understand and accept the people they are leading. They refrain from passing judgment, instead choosing to listen, understand, and guide.

As Martin Luther King Jr. once said,

"Love is the only force capable of transforming an enemy into a friend."

In the professional realm, not passing judgment fosters a culture of respect and understanding. It encourages open communication, promotes diversity, and leads to better problem-solving. It allows for the growth and development of individuals and the organization as a whole.

Not passing judgment is a principle that we should all strive to live by. It fosters understanding, acceptance, and love, and it is a mark of great leadership.

Call to Action

Let us strive to live our lives free of judgment. Let us seek to understand before being understood. Let us lead with love and acceptance.

And let us remember the words of Jesus in the book of John, "Judge not, that you be not judged."

Exercises

1. Reflect on a time when you passed judgment on someone. How did it affect your relationship with that person? How could the situation have been different if you had not passed judgment?
2. Think about a leader you admire. How do they demonstrate the principle of not passing judgment?

3.   In your daily interactions, practice active listening. Try to understand the other person's perspective before forming an opinion.

4.   Write down any judgments you find yourself making throughout the day. At the end of the day, reflect on why you made these judgments and how you can avoid making them in the future.

5.   Practice empathy. Try to put yourself in the other person's shoes. How would you feel if you were in their situation?

Chapter 18

The Power of Words: Building Up, Not Knocking Down

The power of words cannot be underestimated. They possess the remarkable ability to uplift and empower, but they can also destroy and wound. This chapter underscores the profound impact of words on our lives and the responsibility we carry to use them wisely.

As shared in my previous stories, I have personally experienced the devastating effects of hurtful words that were used to belittle, punish, and disable me. These words, especially during my formative years, left lasting scars on my self-perception and potential. The wounds inflicted by words can be just as debilitating as physical harm, if not more so.

Throughout my life, I have also witnessed the destructive force of words in relationships, where individuals wielded their verbal prowess as weapons. Emotional abuse, often perpetrated through words, can be just as damaging as physical abuse. The saying "sticks and stones may break my bones, but words will never hurt me" couldn't be further from the truth. Words have the power to wound deeply, leaving emotional and psychological scars that may never fully heal.

Tragically, some individuals have been pushed to the brink, even to the point of taking their own lives, as a result of the relentless barrage of hurtful words. In today's digital age, the venomous words of cyberbullying and social media can be equally lethal.

My faith and the teachings of Jesus have been instrumental in shaping my perspective on the power of words. I have been conditioned to use my words to empower and heal the minds and souls of others. I have learned the transformative value of replacing negative self-talk with self-love and empowering affirmations. So profound is this belief that I have permanently etched my most cherished affirmation on my arm: "I can do all things through Christ who strengthens me" (Philippians 4:13). This serves as a constant reminder that I am capable, loved, and empowered.

In our roles as leaders, we carry a tremendous responsibility in wielding the power of words. We have the capacity to either build or destroy, to empower or demean. Our words hold the potential to shape the self-esteem and confidence of those we lead.

It is imperative that we use our tongues not as swords that cut and wound but as instruments that build, encourage, and breathe life into those around us. Let us choose our words wisely, for they hold immeasurable weight and meaning.

The power of words is a profound force that can either build or destroy lives. We must recognize the responsibility we carry in using our words to empower and uplift, for our words possess the potential to heal and transform, not wound and harm.

Main Point

The power of words is a double-edged sword, capable of either building or destroying lives. As leaders, we must use our words wisely, choosing to empower, encourage, and add life to ourselves and others.

Personal Quote

"Words are the threads that weave our stories. Let us choose words that uplift and empower, for our words have the power to build, heal, and transform lives." Giulio Veglio

In the book of John, we find a profound example of the power of words. John, a disciple of Jesus, was known for his eloquent and uplifting words. He used his words to inspire, encourage, and build up those around him. Jesus, too, was a master of words. His teachings, filled with wisdom and love, have influenced billions of people throughout history.

John 1:1 states,

"In the beginning was the Word, and the Word was with God, and the Word was God."

This verse emphasizes the power and significance of words. Words have the power to create, shape reality, and influence people's thoughts, feelings, and actions.

Using words wisely is a responsibility we all share. Words can be used for good or evil, to build up or to knock down. They can inspire or discourage, heal or hurt, create or destroy. As such, it is crucial that we use our words to uplift others, to inspire confidence, and to promote positivity.

In our personal and professional lives, words play a vital role. They can build self-confidence, foster healthy relationships, and inspire us to achieve our goals. Great leaders understand this power. They use their words to inspire their teams, to instill confidence, and to motivate action.

John F. Kennedy once said,

"Leadership and learning are indispensable to each other."

This quote emphasizes the importance of using words for learning and leadership. Leaders who use their words wisely can inspire their teams to learn, grow, and achieve their full potential.

The power of words cannot be underestimated. They have the potential to shape our world, to inspire others, and to create positive change. As leaders, it is our responsibility to use our words wisely, to uplift others, and to inspire action.

Call to Action

Let us commit to using our words for good, to inspire self-confidence in ourselves and others, and to build a better world.

Exercises

1. Reflect on a time when someone's words had a significant impact on you. How did it make you feel? How did it influence your actions?
2. Think about a leader you admire. How do they use their words to inspire and motivate their team?
3. Write down five positive affirmations that you can say to yourself every day to boost your self-confidence.
4. Practice using positive and uplifting language in your daily interactions. Notice how it influences the people around you.
5. Write a letter to someone who has inspired you, thanking them for their positive influence in your life. Use your words to express your gratitude and appreciation.

Chapter 19
Taking Time to Reflect and Refresh

In the hustle and bustle of American life, the concept of relaxation often eluded me during my upbringing. My parents, like many others, worked tirelessly to provide for our family, and their tireless dedication left indelible marks on my impressionable young mind: work, work, and more work.

As a child, I took on multiple paper routes, mowed lawns, and sought any legal opportunity to earn money. This work ethic persisted as I ventured into entrepreneurship at the young age of 21, operating my salon from early morning until midnight or beyond if a client so desired. As my business expanded, my commitment to labor was unyielding, and I found myself incessantly tethered to the phone.

Even as a family man, I remained addicted to work, often squeezing in my children's basketball and baseball games between work-related commitments. During dinner, I would prioritize phone calls over engaging with my own family.

The toll this lifestyle took on my well-being and family life eventually became undeniable. It was during this time that I began to contemplate the concept of the Sabbath—a day of rest that God Himself observed after creating the world in six days. The realization struck me: if even God rested, then so should I.

I used to question why businesses like Chick-Fil-A closed on Sundays when families were more inclined to dine out. I mistakenly believed they were losing out on substantial profits. However, I soon learned that Chick-fil-A's commitment to observing the Sabbath, a day of rest and reflection, did not hinder its success. In fact, the company thrived, outperforming many, if not all, other fast-food chains.

Inspired by this revelation, I made the decision not to work on Sundays, and I extended this practice to my staff as well. We all need at least one day to relax, refresh, and savor precious moments with our loved ones.

Today, I make it a point to set aside time for reflection, relaxation, and renewal every day. I have come to understand that even Jesus, along with His disciples, recognized the importance of taking moments to retreat and refresh. His occasional disappearances were opportunities for reflection, rejuvenation, and reconnection with the divine.

In this chapter, we delve into the significance of rest and renewal, emphasizing the art of finding time for relaxation amidst life's demands. We learn that even the most driven individuals, like Jesus and His disciples, require moments of reflection and reprieve to thrive in their respective missions.

In conclusion, the lesson of this chapter is clear: in the relentless pursuit of our goals and responsibilities, we must never neglect the necessity of rest and renewal. It is in these moments of reflection and relaxation that we find the strength to continue our journey and fully appreciate the beauty of life.

Main Point

Amidst life's demands, we must prioritize rest and renewal. Just as God observed the Sabbath after creating the world, we too must find time for reflection and relaxation to thrive in our journey.

Personal Quote

"In the symphony of life, rest is the pause that allows us to appreciate the music. Embrace moments of reflection and renewal, for they give us the strength to continue our journey with renewed vigor and purpose." Giulio Veglio

In the book of John, there is a profound lesson about the importance of taking time to be alone, to reflect, and to refresh oneself. John, a devoted disciple of Jesus, understood the significance of solitude and introspection. He witnessed firsthand how Jesus would often withdraw from the crowds and find solace in quiet moments of reflection.

John recognized that these moments of solitude were not signs of weakness or isolation but rather opportunities for rejuvenation and self-discovery. Jesus, as a great leader, understood the necessity of alone time to gather his thoughts, seek guidance, and recharge his spirit.

In the Gospel of John, Jesus once said,

"I am the vine; you are the branches. If you remain in me and I in you, you will bear much fruit; apart from me, you can do nothing."

This profound statement emphasizes the importance of staying connected to oneself and finding inner peace through reflection and introspection.

Throughout history, great leaders have echoed this sentiment. Mahatma Gandhi, a transformative figure in India's struggle for independence, once said,

"In the attitude of silence, the soul finds the path in a clearer light, and what is elusive and deceptive resolves itself into crystal clearness."

Reflecting on these teachings, we can apply the same principles to our personal and professional lives. As leaders, it is crucial to carve out moments of solitude to reflect and refresh ourselves. Here are five exercises that can provoke thought and action in our lives:

1. **Morning Meditation:** Begin each day with a few minutes of quiet meditation. Focus on your breath, clear your mind, and set positive intentions for the day ahead. This practice will help you start your day with clarity and purpose.

2. **Nature Walks:** Take regular walks in nature, away from the hustle and bustle of daily life. Allow the beauty of the natural world to inspire and rejuvenate you. Use this time to reflect on your goals, challenges, and aspirations.

3. **Journaling:** Set aside time each day to write in a journal. Reflect on your experiences, emotions, and thoughts. This practice will help you gain insights into yourself and provide a space for self-expression and self-discovery.

4. **Digital Detox:** Disconnect from technology for a designated period each day. Turn off your phone, step away from screens, and embrace the silence. Use this time to reconnect with yourself, free from distractions.

5. **Retreats and Sabbaticals:** Plan regular retreats or sabbaticals to fully immerse yourself in solitude and reflection. These longer periods away from your usual routine will allow for deep introspection, personal growth, and rejuvenation.

As John and Jesus exemplified, taking time to reflect and refresh is not a luxury but a necessity for personal and professional growth. By embracing solitude, we can find clarity, gain insights, and become better leaders. Let us remember the words of John, and prioritize the moments of quiet introspection that lead us to greatness.

"He must increase, but I must decrease."

Chapter 20
Dealing with Rejection: Lessons from John and Jesus

In the pursuit of my entrepreneurial dreams, I often found myself facing rejection, a formidable adversary that can easily discourage and dishearten. The rejection wasn't limited to financial institutions; even friends and family failed to share my vision. At times, it felt as if I was standing alone, my dreams dismissed as foolish.

Rejection, especially when faced repeatedly, has the power to wound one's spirit and provoke self-doubt. It left me questioning whether I was on the wrong path if my ventures were indeed as impractical as others claimed. However, I was fortunate to possess a strength and resilience that compelled me to persist, keep moving forward, and seek alternative avenues to bring my vision to life.

I vividly remember a pivotal moment when I sold my home and all my belongings, uprooting my family for the chance to open a school in Orlando, Florida. Despite my unwavering determination, for two long years, I encountered one obstacle after another. Finding a suitable location proved elusive, and my financial resources dwindled.

But faith and determination sustained me, and I continued to forge ahead. Then, in a remarkable twist of fate, the Lord answered my prayers. After numerous rejections from a landlord who owned multiple properties, he unexpectedly offered me the perfect location—a 23,000-square-foot space in dire need of renovation.

Initially, the cost of the build-out seemed insurmountable, and I was on the brink of rejecting the offer. That's when the landlord proposed a solution that left me in awe. He not only agreed to cover the build-out expenses but also offered an affordable monthly rent, amortized over ten years. It was an answer to my prayers, a provision from above that surpassed my wildest expectations.

This chapter emphasizes the crucial lesson that rejection is not the end of the journey but merely a pause in God's grander plan. Every prior rejection, every obstacle encountered, was part of a divine orchestration leading to a more significant opportunity. God's ways are mysterious, and His plans often far exceed our own.

In conclusion, the message of this chapter is clear: in the face of rejection, do not lose hope or question your dreams. Rejection is merely a detour on the path to God's bigger and better plans. Embrace it as an opportunity for growth and faith in the divine purpose that awaits.

Main Point:

Rejection is not the end of the journey; it is a divine pause leading to greater opportunities in God's grander plan. Trust in His mysterious ways and keep moving forward.

Personal Quote:

"Rejection is not a roadblock; it's a signpost on the path to God's bigger and better plans. Embrace each rejection as a stepping stone to your divine destiny."

"If the world hates you, keep in mind that it hated me first" (John 15:18

In the book of John, we find a profound story of two individuals who faced immense rejection and yet managed to rise above it. John, the beloved disciple, and Jesus, the Son of God, encountered numerous instances of rejection throughout their journey. Their experiences teach us valuable lessons on how to deal with rejection and move forward in life.

Rejection is an inevitable part of life, and it can be disheartening and discouraging. However, it is crucial to understand that rejection does not define our worth or potential. John and Jesus exemplify this truth through their unwavering faith and resilience.

John, known as the disciple whom Jesus loved, faced rejection in various forms. He witnessed Jesus being rejected by his own people, the Pharisees, and even some of his own disciples. Despite this, John remained steadfast in his commitment to Jesus and his teachings. He understood that rejection was not a reflection of his own character but rather a response to the message he carried.

Jesus, the ultimate example of love and compassion, faced rejection on a grand scale. He was rejected by religious leaders, mocked by the crowds, and ultimately crucified. Yet, Jesus never allowed rejection to deter him from his mission. He continued to spread his message of love, forgiveness, and salvation, knowing that his purpose was greater than the opinions of others.

Understanding how to deal with rejection is essential for personal and professional growth. Great leaders, like John and Jesus, recognize that rejection is not fatal. It is merely a stepping stone towards success.

They embrace rejection as an opportunity to learn, grow, and refine their skills.

To effectively handle rejection, leaders can adopt the following practices:

1. **Embrace Resilience:** Develop a resilient mindset that allows you to bounce back from rejection. Remember that rejection is not a reflection of your worth but an opportunity for growth.

2. **Seek Feedback:** Instead of dwelling on rejection, seek feedback from trusted mentors or colleagues. Constructive criticism can help you identify areas for improvement and enhance your skills.

3. **Cultivate Self-Confidence:** Build a strong sense of self-confidence that enables you to withstand rejection. Believe in your abilities and remain focused on your goals, regardless of setbacks.

4. **Practice Self-Reflection:** Take time to reflect on your experiences of rejection. Analyze what went wrong, identify any patterns, and learn from them. Use rejection as a catalyst for personal and professional development.5.Foster Empathy: Understand that rejection is not exclusive to you. Develop empathy towards others who may be experiencing rejection and offer support and encouragement. By doing so, you create a positive and inclusive environment.

As John wrote in his gospel,

"If the world hates you, keep in mind that it hated me first" (John 15:18).

These words remind us that even the greatest leaders faced rejection. However, they overcame it by staying true to their purpose and embracing rejection as a stepping stone towards greatness.

Rejection is an inevitable part of life, but it does not define us. By drawing inspiration from the experiences of John and Jesus, we can learn to deal with rejection effectively. Embrace resilience, seek feedback, cultivate self-confidence, practice self- reflection, and foster empathy. Remember, rejection is not fatal, but rather an opportunity for growth and transformation.

Chapter 21

Crucial Conversations: Lessons from John and Jesus

Throughout my life's journey, I often found myself entangled in crucial conversations, a necessity that stemmed from my tendency to make mistakes, especially in light of my later-diagnosed conditions of ADD, ADHD, and Dyslexia, discovered through assessments with psychiatrists.

Crucial conversations are those moments when the stakes are high, emotions run deep, and differing opinions collide. Such conversations can be intimidating, especially when you've grappled with a history of missteps and misunderstandings. However, I've learned that these conversations can hold profound transformative power, provided they are approached with patience and grace.

Embracing crucial conversations became a turning point in my life. I recognized them as opportunities for growth and self-awareness rather than as hurdles to avoid. Instead of shrinking from these discussions, I learned to lean into them, ready to listen and learn from others' perspectives. In doing so, I gained valuable insights into my own behaviors and triggers, enabling me to better manage my challenges.

Crucial conversations are not limited to personal interactions; they extend into professional and leadership realms as well. As a leader, I've come to appreciate that these conversations often mark the crucible of personal and organizational growth.

This chapter explores the significance of crucial conversations and the transformation they can bring. It underscores the importance of empathy, active listening, and humility when navigating these challenging discussions. The chapter's core message is that by approaching crucial conversations with an open heart and mind, we can foster understanding, empathy, and growth.

In conclusion, this chapter conveys the importance of crucial conversations and their potential to transform relationships and leadership. They offer us the opportunity to rise above personal emotions, prioritize important information, and lead with love and empathy.

Main Point:

Crucial conversations, when handled with grace and empathy, can be transformative opportunities for growth, fostering understanding and harmony, both personally and as a leader.

Personal Quote:

"In the crucible of crucial conversations, empathy and grace become our guiding lights. Approach them with an open heart, and you'll discover the transformative power of understanding and growth."

In the biblical book of John, we find numerous instances of crucial conversations between John, Jesus, and others. These dialogues were not just exchanges of words, but they were purposeful, filled with love, and aimed at transformation.

One of the most profound conversations in the book of John is when Jesus speaks to Nicodemus about being born again (John 3:1-21).

This was a crucial conversation as it challenged Nicodemus's understanding of spiritual rebirth. Jesus, with love and patience, explained the concept, thereby transforming Nicodemus's perspective.

In our personal and professional lives, we often encounter situations that require crucial conversations. These conversations can be challenging, but they are necessary for growth and progress. Great leaders understand the importance of these dialogues and approach them with purpose and love, just as Jesus did.

John 13:34 quotes Jesus saying,

"A new command I give you: Love one another. As I have loved you, so you must love one another."

This quote emphasizes the importance of love in our interactions, including our crucial conversations.

Martin Luther King Jr., a great leader of our time, once said,

"Our lives begin to end the day we become silent about things that matter."

This quote underscores the importance of having crucial conversations, even when they are difficult. Here are five exercises to help you prepare for crucial conversations:

1.   **Self-reflection:** Before the conversation, reflect on your intentions. Are you approaching the conversation with love and a genuine desire for resolution?

2. **Empathy Exercise:** Try to understand the other person's perspective. This will help you approach the conversation with empathy and respect.

3. **Scripture Study:** Reflect on the conversations between Jesus and others in the book of John. What can you learn from these dialogues?

4. **Role-play:** Practice the conversation with a friend or mentor. This can help you prepare for the actual dialogue.

5. **Action Plan:** After the conversation, create an action plan. What steps will you take to address the issue discussed?

Remember, crucial conversations are not about winning an argument but about understanding each other better. Approach them with love, patience, and a willingness to learn, just as Jesus did in his conversations.

Chapter 22

The Power of "I AM"

As a young child, I was captivated by the film "The Ten Commandments," and two words in particular left an indelible mark on me: "I AM." Little did I know that these two simple words would later hold profound significance in my life.

Throughout my journey, I encountered numerous individuals who tried to define me, telling me who I was supposed to be. Unfortunately, their messages were rarely ones of encouragement or empowerment. It took time, self-discovery, and a deep understanding of the significance of "I AM" to redefine my identity.

Understanding the power of these two words, I embarked on a journey of self-discovery. I realized that, as children of God, we are all made in His image and bestowed with unique gifts and potential. These affirmations became my armor, my shield against the negativity and doubt that others sought to impose upon me.

I began to write affirmations that described who I truly am, using uplifting and positive language. This practice not only reinforced my self-worth but also allowed me to stand confidently in my own identity. When you fully embrace and accept who you are, you become a force to be reckoned with, radiating confidence and self-assuredness.

Knowing and accepting your identity is crucial, not only for your own well-being but also as a defense against those who might seek to diminish you. A confident person who believes in themselves is not an easy target for bullies or abusers.

In conclusion, this chapter highlights the transformative power of "I AM." It underscores the importance of understanding and accepting your true identity, unshackling yourself from the limiting beliefs others may try to impose. Embrace who you are with confidence, knowing that you are a unique creation with incredible potential.

Main Point:

The words "I AM" carry immense power. Discovering and accepting your true identity, grounded in positivity and self-worth, is the key to standing confidently in the face of doubt and negativity.

Personal Quote:

"In the presence of 'I AM,' negativity and doubt wither away. Embrace your true identity with confidence, for it is the key to unlocking your boundless potential." Giulio Veglio

Remember the words of John and Jesus, and let the power of

"I AM"

And let it guide you on your path to greatness...

In the book of John, there is a profound emphasis on the power of the words *"I AM."* John, a devoted disciple of Jesus, recognized the significance of these two words in understanding one's identity and purpose. Through their teachings and actions, both John and Jesus exemplified the importance of knowing who they were and standing proudly in their identity.

John, a humble and wise man, understood that his purpose was to prepare the way for Jesus, the Messiah. He knew that he was not the light but a witness to the light. With unwavering conviction, John proclaimed,

"I am the voice of one crying out in the wilderness, 'Make straight the way of the Lord'" (John 1:23).

By acknowledging who he was and his role in God's plan, John embraced his purpose and carried it out with great pride.

Jesus, the Son of God, also recognized the power of *"I AM."* Throughout his ministry, he used these words to reveal his divine nature and to teach others about their own identities.

Jesus boldly declared,

"I am the bread of life; whoever comes to me shall not hunger" (John 6:35)

&

"I am the light of the world. Whoever follows me will not walk in darkness but will have the light of life" (John 8:12).

By using these words, Jesus not only asserted his identity but also invited others to find their true selves in him.

Understanding who we are and standing proudly in our identity is crucial in both personal and professional lives. Great leaders throughout history have recognized this truth.

Mahatma Gandhi once said,

"Be the change that you wish to see in the world."

This quote emphasizes the importance of knowing oneself and being proud of one's values and beliefs. When leaders have a clear understanding of their identity, they can inspire and guide others towards positive change.

To help you embrace the power of *"I AM"* in your personal and professional life, here are five exercises to provoke thoughts and create an action plan:

1. **Self-Reflection:** Take time to reflect on your values, strengths, and passions. Write down the qualities that define who you are and what you stand for.

2. **Affirmations:** Create positive affirmations starting with "I AM." Repeat these affirmations daily to reinforce your self-belief and confidence.

3. **Purpose Alignment:** Align your personal and professional goals with your core values. Ensure that your actions and decisions reflect who you truly are.

4. **Authenticity:** Embrace your uniqueness and be true to yourself. Avoid trying to fit into societal expectations or imitating others. Celebrate your individuality.

5. **Inspiring Others:** Use your own journey of self-discovery to inspire and empower others. Encourage them to explore their identities and embrace their strengths.

By confidently using the words "I AM" and understanding your true self, you can become a great leader who inspires and positively impacts those around you. Remember the words of John and Jesus, and let the power of "I AM" guide you on your path to greatness.

Chapter 23
Choosing FAITH over FEAR

In life, we are faced with a pivotal choice: to embrace faith or succumb to fear. I have always chosen faith, as fear has the power to imprison the mind and prevent us from fully enjoying the abundant life that awaits.

At the tender age of twenty, I was introduced to a cassette tape by the renowned motivational speaker Zig Ziglar. This was my first encounter with the world of motivational tapes and seminars, an eye-opening experience that would shape my perspective on life.

Among the many pearls of wisdom shared by Ziglar, one concept stood out: the idea that fear could be spelled as "F>E>A>R," which stood for "False Evidence Appearing Real." In essence, fear is often an illusion, a product of our imagination that paralyzes us.

In contrast to fear, the word that resonated with me most was "Faith." I chose to always embrace faith, and I even gave it my own meaning, which I share in my seminars: "F.A.I.T.H," representing "Fierce Attitude In The Heart." Faith, is something we can't see with our eyes, but we trust it's there. Just as we trust in the air we breathe, we can trust in the power of faith.

The question of believing in something unseen often arises, whether it's faith or fear. My response is simple: we can't see air or oxygen, yet we unquestionably trust in their existence as we continue to breathe. Faith, for me, has proven to be a guiding force, propelling me further in life than fear ever could.

In conclusion, this chapter highlights the critical choice between faith and fear. By choosing faith, we unlock the door to a world of possibilities and break free from the chains of fear's illusion.

Main Point:

In life, we must make a conscious choice between faith and fear. Faith, with its unwavering belief and fierce attitude in the heart, has the power to propel us forward and break the shackles of fear's illusion.

Personal Quote:

"Choose faith over fear, for faith is the fierce attitude in your heart that will propel you beyond the illusions of fear." - Giulio Veglio

"I can do all things through Christ who strengthens me" Philippians 4:13.

In the Biblical book of John, there are numerous instances where Jesus and John converse about the importance of faith over fear. One of the most profound is when Jesus says,

"Do not let your hearts be troubled. Trust in God; trust also in me" (John 14:1).

This statement is a clear testament to the power of faith, a call to trust in the divine plan, and a reminder not to let fear cloud our judgment or actions.

Zig Ziglar, a renowned motivational speaker, once said

"That fear is spelled F.E.A.R., which stands for False Evidence Appearing Real."

This means that fear is often based on things that aren't real or haven't happened yet. It's a projection of our anxieties onto the future, a future that is uncertain and largely unknown.

On the other hand, Giulio Veglio, a renowned Speaker and Educator, defines faith as:

"F.A.I.T.H., or Fierce Attitude in the Heart."

This implies that faith is a strong, unwavering belief in our hearts, a conviction that guides us through life's challenges and uncertainties.

In our personal and professional lives, choosing faith over fear can be transformative. It can lead to better decision-making, improved relationships, and increased resilience. Great leaders, in particular, understand the importance of faith. They know that fear can paralyze them, but faith can empower them. As Martin Luther King Jr. once said,

"Faith is taking the first step even when you don't see the whole staircase."

Here are five exercises to help you choose faith over fear:

1. **Reflection:** Reflect on a time when fear held you back and a time when faith propelled you forward. What were the outcomes of both situations?

2. **Visualization:** Visualize your fears. Now, visualize overcoming them. How does that make you feel?

3. **Affirmation:** Write down affirmations that reinforce your faith and read them daily. For example, "I have the power to overcome my fears."

4. **Action:** Identify one fear that's holding you back. What's one step you can take today to overcome it?

5. **Gratitude:** Practice gratitude. Being thankful for what you have can help you focus on the positives and strengthen your faith.

You can choose to believe in fear, which can hold you back, or you can choose to have faith, which can propel you forward. As it is written in the Book of John,

"I have told you these things, so that in me you may have peace. In this world you will have trouble. But take heart! I have overcome the world" (John 16:33).

Choosing faith over fear will not only bring you peace but also great Joy.

Chapter 24
Being a Vine Dresser

"I am the vine; you are the branches. If you remain in me and I in you, you will bear much fruit; apart from me, you can do nothing" (John 15:5).

Once upon a time, in a small village nestled between the hills and the river, lived a farmer named Samuel. Samuel was a hardworking man, but he had a flaw - he neglected his fields. He owned a vast expanse of land, fertile and rich, but he didn't pay much attention to its upkeep. He didn't prune the trees, didn't remove the weeds, and didn't eliminate the dead branches. His fields were a sight of chaos and neglect.

The crops grew, but they were weak and sparse. The fruit trees bore fruit, but they were small and sour. The weeds choked the life out of the plants, and the dead branches blocked the sunlight. Samuel's harvest was poor, and he barely made enough to sustain his family.

One day, a wise old man from the village visited Samuel. He looked at the fields and shook his head. "Samuel," he said, "Your land is rich and fertile. It can give you a bountiful harvest, but you must tend to it. You must prune the trees, remove the weeds, and eliminate the dead branches."

Samuel listened to the old man's words. He realized his mistake and decided to change his ways. The very next day, he woke up at dawn and started working on his fields. He pruned the trees, removing the dead and diseased branches. He pulled out the weeds, freeing the crops from their choking grasp. He worked tirelessly, day after day, tending to his fields with care and dedication.

Slowly but surely, the fields started to change. The crops grew stronger and healthier. The fruit trees bore bigger and sweeter fruits. The weeds were gone, and the sunlight reached every corner of the field. Samuel's hard work was paying off.

When the harvest season came, Samuel reaped a bountiful harvest. His crops were the best in the village, and his fruits were the sweetest. He made a good profit, enough to sustain his family and save for the future. His fields were a sight of beauty and prosperity.

From then on, Samuel never neglected his fields. He tended to them with care and diligence, pruning the trees, removing the weeds, and eliminating the dead branches. His fields gave him a bountiful harvest year after year, and he lived a prosperous and happy life.

The story of Samuel teaches us the importance of diligence and care. Just like the fields, our lives can bear great fruit if we tend to them with care and dedication. Neglect and carelessness can lead to poor results, but hard work and diligence can lead to prosperity and success.

Now you can be the Vine Dresser you were made to be as we read What a Vine Dress is from John and Jesus protective and how it relates to us personally and professionally.

In the book of John, there is a profound conversation between John and Jesus about the concept of being a vinedresser. Jesus uses this analogy to illustrate the importance of tending to our personal and professional lives, just as a vine dresser tends to a vineyard, protecting it from weeds and dead branches to ensure it bears great fruit.

John, eager to understand this analogy, asks Jesus why it is crucial to protect and nurture our vine, both in our personal lives and as leaders in business. Jesus responds with wisdom,

"I am the vine; you are the branches. If you remain in me and I in you, you will bear much fruit; apart from me, you can do nothing" (John 15:5).

Reflecting on this profound statement, John realizes that just as a vine needs constant care and attention to flourish, our lives and businesses require the same level of dedication. Neglecting our personal growth or allowing negative influences to hinder our progress can stunt our potential and limit our ability to bear fruit.

Drawing inspiration from Jesus' teachings, John explores how this analogy applies to our personal and professional lives, particularly for those aspiring to be great leaders. He delves into the wisdom of both biblical quotes and quotes from renowned leaders who understand the significance of tending to the harvest and protecting it.

To help readers apply these principles, This presents five thought-provoking exercises and an action plan for your personal and professional lives as leaders:

1. **Reflect on Your Purpose:** Take time to deeply understand your purpose in life and in your business. Align your actions and decisions with this purpose to ensure growth and fulfillment.

2. **Weed Out Negativity:** Identify and eliminate negative influences in your life and business. Surround yourself with positive and supportive individuals who encourage your growth and success.

3.   **Prune Dead Branches:** Regularly assess your personal and professional life to identify areas that are no longer serving you. Let go of outdated practices, habits, or relationships that hinder your progress.

4.   **Nurture Growth:** Invest in continuous learning and personal development. Seek opportunities to expand your knowledge, skills, and perspectives to foster growth in both your personal and professional life.

5.   **Cultivate a Supportive Environment:** Build a team or network of individuals who share your vision and values. Foster a culture of collaboration, trust, and support to create an environment that nurtures growth and success.

Being a vine dresser is not only a Biblical concept but also a powerful metaphor for our personal and professional lives. By tending to our growth, protecting ourselves from negative influences, and nurturing our potential, we can bear great fruit and become effective leaders.

As John concludes this chapter, he emphasizes the importance of embracing the role of a vine dresser in our lives, ensuring that we run and protect what we have planted for our life and business, ultimately leading to a fruitful and fulfilling journey.

Chapter 25
The Paradox of Pain and Joy

Pain is an inevitable thread that weaves its way through. However, what we choose to do with that pain is entirely within our control, guided by our faith in God and Jesus Christ. I have faced my fair share of pain, but I have also come to intimately know the profound depths of joy.

Life's journey guarantees that we will encounter pain, but how we respond to it is where the power lies. When confronted with pain, I turn to my unwavering faith in God and Jesus Christ, trusting in their guidance to lead me from the depths of despair to the pinnacle of joy. The choice is ours: we can choose to dwell in perpetual suffering, or we can take action.

I have witnessed the loss of dear friends to various diseases such as cancer, AIDS, drunk driving accidents, and the COVID-19 pandemic. Each loss brought with it an initial wave of excruciating pain, but I refused to allow that pain to consume me. Instead, I turned my pain into purpose.

I became proactive, dedicating my efforts to raising funds for cancer research, supporting AIDS awareness initiatives, and advocating for responsible drinking practices through organizations like Mothers Against Drunk Driving.

Additionally, I delved into studying the COVID-19 pandemic at Johns Hopkins University, equipping myself with the knowledge to protect my staff, students, and guests when we reopened our establishments with safety protocols that exceeded even the health department's guidelines.

In life, we face a choice when confronted with pain: we can remain victims or rise to the challenge, becoming catalysts for positive change. By actively seeking solutions and embracing a mindset of service, we not only bring joy into our lives but also illuminate the lives of countless others.

Main Point:

Pain is an inevitable part of life, but our response to it is a choice. By turning our pain into purpose and taking action, we can bring joy not only into our own lives but also into the lives of those around us.

Personal Quote:

"In the face of pain, we have a choice: to be victims or victors. Let your pain be the catalyst for positive change and the source of boundless joy." - Giulio Veglio

In the book of John, there is a profound conversation between Jesus and his disciple, John. Jesus said,

"In this world, you will have trouble. But take heart! I have overcome the world" (John 16:33).

This statement encapsulates the essence of life's duality - pain and joy.

As humans, we are bound to experience pain. It is an inevitable part of our existence. However, suffering is a choice. We can choose to dwell in our pain, or we can choose to transform it into joy. This principle applies not only to our personal lives but also to our professional lives as leaders.

Consider the story of a woman about to give birth. The pain she endures during labor is intense, almost unbearable. Yet, the moment she holds her newborn in her arms, all the pain dissipates, replaced by overwhelming joy. This is a powerful analogy for leadership. Leaders often face challenges and difficulties, but the joy of achieving their goals makes the journey worthwhile.

John 16:21 says,

"A woman giving birth to a child has pain because her time has come; but when her baby is born she forgets the anguish because of her joy that a child is born into the world."

This quote is a testament to the transformative power of joy over pain.

Great leaders understand this principle. They know that the path to success is often paved with difficulties. Yet, they also know that these challenges are opportunities for growth.

As Winston Churchill once said,

"The pessimist sees difficulty in every opportunity. The optimist sees the opportunity in every difficulty."

Here are five exercises to provoke thought and create an action plan for turning pain into joy in your personal and professional life:

1.   Identify a recent challenge you faced. How did it make you feel? How did you overcome it? What joy did you find in the resolution?

2.   Reflect on a time when you transformed a painful experience into a joyful one. What steps did you take? How can you apply this process to future challenges?

3.   Write down your biggest fear as a leader. Now, write down three ways you can turn this fear into an opportunity for growth.

4.   Think about a painful experience you're currently facing. How can you shift your perspective to see the potential joy in this situation?

5.   Create an action plan for the next challenge you face. How will you approach it? How will you find joy in the journey?

Pain and joy are two sides of the same coin. As leaders, we will face pain, but we have the power to transform it into joy. As we tend to our personal and professional lives, like a farmer tending to his harvest, we must protect and nurture what we've planted. In doing so, we can turn even the most painful experiences into opportunities for joy and growth. The main point of this chapter is to inspire leaders to embrace the paradox of pain and joy and to use it as a catalyst for personal and professional growth.

The Final Chapter
The Closing

As we draw the curtains on this enlightening journey through the lives of John and Jesus, it is important to reflect on the profound lessons we have learned. This book is not just a collection of stories, but a guide, a beacon of light that illuminates the path of righteousness and love. It is a testament to the power of living by example, as demonstrated by John and Jesus, whose lives were the epitome of selfless love, unwavering faith, and steadfast commitment to their divine missions.

John and Jesus did not merely preach; they lived their teachings, leading by example. Their lives were a testament to the power of faith, love, and service. They showed us that true leadership is not about power or control, but about serving others with love and humility.

One of the most profound quotes from the Bible that encapsulates this is from the book of John, chapter 13, verse 15:

"I have set you an example that you should do as I have done for you."

This quote is a powerful reminder that we are called to live our lives in service to others, just as Jesus did.

Another quote that speaks volumes about leading a faith-filled life is from 1 John 4:16:

"And so we know and rely on the love God has for us. God is love. Whoever lives in love lives in God, and God in them."

This quote reminds us that love is the essence of our faith, and it is through love that we can truly connect with God and others.

These chapters are not just stories to be read once and forgotten. They are a source of wisdom and knowledge that we can refer back to in times of need. They are a guide to living a life filled with love, faith, and service. They remind us that we are not alone in our journey and that we have a divine guide in the form of the teachings of John and Jesus.

In our personal and professional lives, these teachings can shape our actions and decisions. They can guide us in our interactions with others, helping us to lead with love and humility. They can inspire us to live our lives with purpose and intention, always striving to serve others and make a positive impact on the world.

Let us remember the words of John 13:34,

"A new command I give you: Love one another. As I have loved you, so you must love one another."

Let this be our guiding principle as we navigate the complexities of life, always striving to live with love, faith, and intention. Let the lives of John and Jesus be our guide, inspiring us to lead by example and make a positive difference in the world.

May God bless you all as you continue to live in His name.

Here's a list of books that I would recommend for someone seeking tolive a godly life in today's world:

1. **The Bible**: The primary source of Christian teachings, the Bible is a must-read for anyone seeking to live a godly life. It provides guidance, wisdom, and inspiration.

2. **"Jesus CEO: Using Ancient Wisdom for Visionary Leadership" by Laurie Beth Jones**: This book takes the teachings of Jesus and applies them to modern business leadership. It's a great read for anyone looking to lead with integrity and compassion.

3. **"Traveling Light" by Max Lucado**: Lucado uses the 23rd Psalm as a guide to show readers how to release the burdens they were never intended to bear.

4. **"The 21 Irrefutable Laws of Leadership" by John C. Maxwell**: Maxwell, a Christian author, offers principles of leadership that can help you in all areas of life.

5. **"Just As I Am: The Autobiography of Billy Graham" by Billy Graham**: This autobiography provides a glimpse into the life of one of the most influential Christian leaders of the 20th century.

6. **"The Purpose Driven Life: What on Earth Am I Here For?" by Rick Warren**: This book offers readers a 40-day personal spiritual journey, and presents what Warren says are God's five purposes for human life on Earth.

7. **"Mere Christianity" by C.S. Lewis**: This book is a classic of Christian apologetics, aiming to explain the fundamental teachings of Christianity.

Made in the USA
Columbia, SC
12 September 2024

41679499R10074